Of Corsets and Secrets and True True Love

Also available in the Road to Avonlea series from Bantam Skylark books

Of Corsets and Secrets and True True Love

Storybook written by

Fiona McHugh

Based on the Sullivan Films Production
written by Marlene Matthews
adapted from the novels of

Lucy Maud Montgomery

Athens Regional Library
2025 Baxter Street
Athens, GA 30606

A BANTAM SKYLARK BOOK®
TORONTO · NEW YORK · LONDON · SYDNEY · AUCKLAND

MADISON COUNTY LIBRARY
P.O. BOX 38
DANIELSVILLE, GA 30633-0038

Based on the Sullivan Films Production produced by Sullivan Films Inc.
in association with CBC and the Disney Channel with the participation
of Telefilm Canada adapted from Lucy Maud Montgomery's novels.

Teleplay written by Marlene Matthews.
Copyright © 1991 by Sullivan Films Distribution, Inc.

This edition contains the complete text
of the original hardcover edition.
NOT ONE WORD HAS BEEN OMITTED.

RL 6, 008–012

OF CORSETS AND SECRETS AND TRUE, TRUE LOVE

A Bantam Skylark Book / published by arrangement with
HarperCollins Publishers Ltd.

PUBLISHING HISTORY
HarperCollins edition published 1992
Bantam edition / May 1993

ROAD TO AVONLEA is the trademark of Sullivan Films Inc.

Skylark Books is a registered trademark of Bantam Books,
a division of Bantam Doubleday Dell Publishing Group, Inc.
Registered in U.S. Patent and Trademark Office and elsewhere.

All rights reserved.
Storybook written by Fiona McHugh.
Copyright © 1992 by HarperCollins Publishers, Sullivan Films
Distribution, Inc., and Ruth Macdonald and David Macdonald.
No part of this book may be reproduced or transmitted
in any form or by any means, electronic or mechanical,
including photocopying, recording, or by any information
storage and retrieval system, without permission in
writing from the publisher.
For information address: HarperCollins Publishers Ltd., Suite 2900,
Hazelton Lanes, 55 Avenue Road, Toronto, Canada M5R 3L2.

If you purchased this book without a cover you should be aware
that this book is stolen property. It was reported as "unsold and
destroyed" to the publisher and neither the author nor the publisher has received any payment for this "stripped book."

ISBN 0-553-48040-5

Bantam Books are published by Bantam Books, a division of Bantam
Doubleday Dell Publishing Group, Inc. Its trademark, consisting of the
words "Bantam Books" and the portrayal of a rooster, is Registered in
U.S. Patent and Trademark Office and in other countries. Marca
Registrada. Bantam Books, 1540 Broadway, New York, New York
10036.

PRINTED IN THE UNITED STATES OF AMERICA

OPM   0 9 8 7 6 5 4 3 2 1

Chapter One

A wasp, it seemed, had nested right under Rachel Lynde's left molar. It buzzed and rasped against the nerve, jangling her brains. She stood still inside the front door, dressed in her funeral finery. Outside, Marilla waited. Marilla disliked waiting, Rachel knew. She knew she should just turn the handle and walk out to the buggy. But she could not move. Pain held her prisoner. Inside her jaw, the wasp jiggled and quivered, as though anxious to be gone. With a little moan, Rachel opened her mouth. No wasp flew out. Rachel slid to a sitting position on the hall chair and closed her eyes. The pain droned on.

The morning sun slanted down on Marilla Cuthbert as she sat, ramrod straight, in the old leather-lined buggy. From where she sat, she could smell the roses twined around the veranda trellis. They were late-blooming roses, lush and full-bodied, at their peak of perfection. Against the dark-green velvet of their leaves, drops of dew glistened like rare jewels not yet stolen by the long-fingered sun. The brown mare stamped her feet and edged closer to the fragrant blossoms, her harness jingling. Angling her head upwards, she nipped a cluster of petals in her yellow teeth and wrenched them off the branch. Marilla made no move to protect her favorite flowers. While the horse chewed on rose after rose, Marilla sat straight as a pole, and worried about Mary Keith.

She had always liked Mary, a smiling, spirited slip of a thing. Now Mary was dead, dead at the unlikely age of twenty-four. It was her funeral they would be late for, if Rachel Lynde didn't hurry. Marilla shifted and blinked her eyes. She hated to be late for any occasion, but to be late for a funeral seemed the height of bad manners. Perhaps she should go in this minute and fetch Rachel. But instead, she sat on in the buggy, breathing in the roses, feeling the sun warm on her shoulders, thinking about poor Mary cold in her grave.

So absorbed was Marilla in her thoughts that she failed to notice Olivia King approaching with Sara

Stanley. Ever since her arrival in Avonlea, the imaginative Sara had reminded Marilla strongly of her own Anne Shirley. Unlike Anne, who had been an orphan, Sara came from a wealthy background, but there was something in her eyes that spoke directly to Marilla's heart. "That child is hungry for love," she had thought the day she first laid eyes on Sara.

Now, catching sight of Miss Cuthbert, Sara ran towards the buggy. "Don't startle her, Sara," warned Olivia under her breath, for even at a distance, she could see Marilla was engrossed in her own thoughts. But Sara had already bounded cheerfully up to the older woman and taken her hand in greeting.

"Good morning, Miss Cuthbert," she beamed. "I hope you don't mind my asking, but do you have any particular talents?"

Olivia King felt like dropping the heavy camera she was carrying on her niece's toe. When would Sara learn to express things a little more diplomatically? But Miss Cuthbert's worn face merely creased into a smile. She had grown used to undiplomatic questions during her years with Anne. In fact, exasperating as they had been at the time, she had to admit she missed those questions now.

"Why, no, I don't believe I possess any particular talents, apart from making the best blueberry pie on the Island." And coping with Rachel Lynde, Marilla refrained from adding.

"Sara and I are doing some research into talented, artistic people in Avonlea, Miss Cuthbert," explained Olivia. "It's for the Avonlea *Chronicle*."

"I don't suppose you ever danced? As a girl, I mean?" Sara eyed Miss Cuthbert's ample form doubtfully.

"I'm afraid I was born with two left feet," smiled Marilla. "But Mrs. Lynde, now, she had quite a voice in her day."

"Rachel Lynde can sing?" asked Olivia, making no attempt to disguise her amazement.

"Why, yes. In fact, Rachel started the first church choir in Avonlea."

"You see, Aunt Olivia? I was right all along. Asking questions really is the best way to find things out. Let's go talk to Mrs. Lynde immediately. Maybe she'll let you take her photograph." Already Sara was halfway up the veranda steps.

"I'm afraid that won't be possible, ladies." Marilla glanced at the little watch pinned to her black jacket. "Mrs. Lynde and I are expected at a funeral, Mary Keith's funeral, for which we are already inexcusably late. Why don't you come back some other day? I'm sure Mrs. Lynde would be happy to share her musical memories over a cup of tea."

"Of course, Miss Cuthbert. I don't know how I

could have forgotten. Hetty told me about Mary Keith. You were related, weren't you?"

"Not closely, but we were still family. She was married to my third cousin, a Cuthbert on his mother's side. I was very fond of poor Mary."

"I'm so sorry, Miss Cuthbert. Please accept our condolences. Come along now, Sara."

With a polite nod, Olivia ushered her niece off down the lane. Marilla was almost sorry to see them go. For a moment, they had distracted her from her worries.

From inside the house, she heard the grandfather clock chime ten. Good heavens, Mary's funeral would be over before they arrived! Getting down from the buggy, Marilla tied the reins firmly around the apple tree next to the veranda and mounted the steps. That familiar mixture of exasperation and fondness that Marilla had come to associate with Rachel Lynde rose again inside her.

When Rachel had come to live at Green Gables after Anne's departure, Marilla had been grateful for her company, but there had always been a lingering doubt in her mind as to the wisdom of the arrangement. After all, the two of them were as different as chalk and cheese. For one thing, Marilla liked to keep her own counsel, while Rachel could talk the hind leg off a donkey. No, there was no denying it: Rachel

Lynde and Marilla Cuthbert were polar opposites. The wonder of it was that they had managed to get along together for such a long time. On days like today, though, when Rachel displayed such an annoying lack of consideration, the suspicion sneaked into Marilla's mind that she might be better off living on her own. She knew such feelings were disloyal, but she could not help having them all the same. In a way, she blamed Rachel for forcing her to think them.

Churning with righteous indignation, Marilla approached the screen door. What in heaven's name could Rachel be up to in there?

Chapter Two

For some time, Rachel had been dimly aware of voices outside. Under normal circumstances, the faintest trace of a voice would have been enough to send her leaping to the window, aquiver with curiosity. The self-appointed watchdog of the community, Rachel felt that to allow any visit to go unrecorded was to sully her reputation as the eyes and ears of Avonlea. Today, however, she felt only the merest flicker of interest. All her energy was concentrated on coping with the pain in her tooth. Surely a wasp *must* be responsible for that buzzing, stinging feeling!

Rachel slid sideways in her seat and peered into the hall mirror. Opening her jaw wide as the St. Lawrence estuary, she stuck out her tongue. The landscape of her mouth startled her. Teeth leaned against each other in clumps, like a rickety picket fence, set in gums redder than Prince Edward Island soil. In the background loomed her tonsils, two wobbly, scarlet mountains. There was no wasp to be seen. But even as she looked, another current of pain flashed like sheet lightning through her sore tooth. The gum beneath it stood out from the rest of her mouth, a livid, unhealthy white. Tears of self-pity started to Rachel's eyes. Even the sight of her best funeral hat, perched atop her head, could not distract her from such discomfort.

"Rachel Lynde, what in heaven's name do you think you're doing? Pulling faces at yourself in the mirror, while I wait outside stuck up on that buggy like Patience on a monument?"

Rachel clamped her mouth shut, almost clipping off a piece of her tongue. Marilla stood in the doorway, her face flushed with anger.

"If you don't get a move on, poor Mary will be under the sod before I have a chance to say my goodbyes."

"Laws, Marilla, if this tooth of mine gets any worse, the next funeral you go to will be my own," retorted Rachel. "And then you'll be sorry you didn't show a little more tolerance towards one in pain." With a martyred sigh, she swept out the door and down to the waiting buggy.

Marilla bit back an angry retort. Truth to tell, Rachel did look a little poorly. Closing the door, she followed her friend outside. As she climbed into the carriage and set the horse in motion, Marilla reproached herself for letting impatience cloud her judgment. Why could she not treat Rachel with a little more charity? After all, charity begins at home. The familiar words reminded Marilla of the problem that had been nagging at her all morning. Like a homing pigeon sighting its nest, her thoughts returned once again to Mary Keith. The problem was not Mary, God rest her soul, but rather what Mary had left behind.

Everyone had been surprised when Mary Norris, laughing Mary, as she was known, with the wide, gray eyes, had married Kenneth Keith. Not that there was anything wrong with Kenneth. It was just that he was at least twice Mary's age and a shy, retiring man. The sort of man, as Rachel put it, who seemed to have more interest in horses than in women. "Better he stick to his horses than be making sheep's eyes after young girls," Rachel Lynde had sniffed when she heard of their engagement. "He'll live to rue the day he chose a child for a bride. You mark my words, Marilla."

But Rachel had been wrong. The marriage had been a sound one. And when, a year later, Kenneth's young wife had presented him with twins, their happiness seemed complete.

Then, out of the blue, tragedy struck. While clearing a piece of land near the back of his farm, Kenneth had been hit by a falling tree. He had died instantly.

Prostrated by grief, his widow had done her best to raise the two small children on her own, but the struggle proved too much for her. Never strong to begin with, she seemed to grow weaker each year. A bad cough, neglected, deteriorated into consumption. The last time Marilla had been to visit, poor Mary had barely been able to draw breath.

Marilla shook her head, as though trying to dismiss the memory. But it persisted. Once again, she saw the dim, airless sickroom, from which all comfort seemed to have fled. Under the thin sheet, Mary's wasted body seemed helpless as a child's. From time to time the hands lying by her side opened and closed spasmodically, as though to grasp the air which evaded her lungs. Outside in the yard, someone was singing, Marilla never knew who. It may have been one of the many children of Mrs. Wiggins, Mary's neighbor. The high, clear voice rose and fell in the quiet room, an unconscious, cruel reminder of the rich life flowing on everywhere but there.

Throughout the visit, Mary had fixed her huge, gray eyes pleadingly on Marilla. She wanted to ask something, Marilla could tell, but the words seemed locked in her throat, prisoners of her failing breath. Marilla had sat on, as twilight thickened into darkness, patting Mary's hand and feeling helpless.

Why? She wondered. Why should death choose a young woman like Mary, with two small children dependent on her? Why should death take her and spare Marilla, an elderly spinster who seemed to have outlived her usefulness? She tried to dismiss these thoughts, which she felt to be somehow blasphemous, but they crouched there in the back of her mind, refusing to go away.

Once, just before Marilla stood up to light the lamp, a little girl had run sobbing into the room and flung herself at her mother's bed. A light flared into life then in Mary's face. A ghost of the laughter from former days shone in her eyes. Placing a thin, almost transparent hand on the child's head, she had looked directly at Marilla. "Do as I ask," she seemed to be saying. "Please, do as I ask."

Marilla had leaned forward. "What is it you're asking, Mary?" she whispered. But at that moment, Mrs. Wiggins bustled into the room, to carry the little girl away to bed. The light went out of Mary's face. The gray eyes closed. A day later she was dead.

Marilla had said nothing to anyone of her

thoughts on that day. She managed to pretend, even to herself, that she had no idea what Mary, with such mute eloquence, had been asking. Deep down, she knew only too well.

The buggy rattled along the quiet lanes, raising angry spurts of red dust. Marilla's face was sternly set. She seemed unaware of the speed at which they were traveling. Beside her, Rachel clutched at her head. Despite her discomfort, she had been looking forward to showing off the new black satin ribbon trimming her funeral hat. She had no desire to lose it before they even reached the cemetery.

"I'll thank you not to drive quite so fast, Marilla," she complained, "You're causing a terrible draught. A person in my condition could catch a chill from that draught. Mary Keith caught a chill and look what happened to her."

"Mary Keith died of consumption. It had nothing to do with a draught."

"Galloping consumption starts with a chill. Chills come from draughts. Everything is foreordained, Marilla. I always said that Mary Keith would die young and die she did. Them skinny kind of girls is the first to perish."

"In that case, Rachel, *you* have nothing to fret about. *You're* doomed to live to a ripe old age."

Rachel felt hurt. The martyred look crept over her face once more.

"I wouldn't count on having me around much longer, Marilla. This tooth is a visitation from Providence, that's what it is. It's a sign that the end is near."

Just as she spoke, the buggy rounded a corner. As if confirming Rachel's words of foreboding, the cemetery stretched out before them.

Chapter Three

Dora and Davy Keith stood by their mother's open grave. When you are seven years old, death is a hard concept to grasp. One minute their mother had been lying quietly in bed. The next minute, people had come and put her in a box. Now everyone was patting the children's heads and saying how sorry they were. If they were so darned sorry, wondered Davy, why couldn't they just give her back?

Never in his whole life had Davy been the focus of so much attention from strangers, yet he would have been happier if they had stopped staring at him and thought about his mother instead. They acted as though they'd forgotten all about her. It seemed clear to Davy that she must be sick and tired of lying in that narrow box. She must be about ready to climb out and come home, he thought. But instead of letting her out, they were lowering the box deep into a terrible black hole. Suddenly he could not bear it a moment longer.

"Hey, don't put my Mama down there! She ain't too good at climbin'. How's she gonna get out?" Davy yelled, rushing forward to the edge of the grave.

Mrs. Wiggins yanked him back. "Didn't I tell you yer Mama had gone to heaven, child?" she snapped. "She ain't never comin back."

Could this be true, Davy wondered? He was not inclined to place too much credence in anything Mrs. Wiggins said. After all, she had sworn black and blue she'd give him a candy if he agreed to put on his horrid black shoes, the ones that pinched his toes. As fast as he could, he had struggled into those leather prisons, but not a glimpse had he caught of the candy.

Beside him, Dora sniffed and tugged at his hand. As the elder, by five minutes, Davy felt responsible for his twin sister. He was darned if he'd let anybody other than himself pull her hair or call her names. Without letting go of her hand, he rummaged in his pocket, found their shared handkerchief and passed it to her. A warm feeling swept over him. In feeling for the handkerchief, his fingers had encountered something even more comforting. He would give it to his Mama. It would stop her being bored, at least for a little while. By then, he might have figured out a way to help her climb up out of that hole.

As Marilla hurried into the cemetery, she caught sight of two small figures standing forlornly by the grave. She made straight towards them. Rachel struggled to keep up, her attention centered not on the children but on the simple casket being lowered into the hole.

"Why, that casket's only pine!" she gasped. "Can you imagine? A body could get slivers just laying in it. Now isn't that a shameful way to meet your Maker, Marilla?"

Marilla paid no attention. Quickening her steps, she approached the children and bent down to put her arms around them. Dora was sobbing quietly into a handkerchief that was none too clean. "There, there, child. Don't cry," she soothed. But the genuine warmth in her voice only made Dora cry harder.

As Marilla turned to Davy, he slipped away from her and ran towards the grave. Before anyone could stop him, he had flung something from his pocket down into the grave. It landed on the coffin with a soft plop.

"Gracious Providence, get that frog outta yer mother's grave!" screamed Mrs. Wiggins, aiming a slap in Davy's direction.

"She needs it. She ain't got nothin' to play with down there." Lying flat on his stomach, Davy reached down to stroke the frog.

Marilla pulled him gently to his feet. "Your mother's in heaven now, Davy. She'll have plenty to play with up there."

Tears rushed to Davy's eyes. "Everyone keeps sayin' up there, up there. But those men dropped her *down*. I saw 'em. How's she gonna get back *up*? I want to know!"

Before Marilla could answer, Mrs. Wiggins had delivered a smart clip to the boy's left ear. Reaching down, she grabbed hold of both children.

"I've had about enough of yer lip, young man. Come along home, now, the pair of you!"

"I don't want your home. I want mine. And I want my Mama," sobbed Dora.

Marilla forced herself to speak calmly. "Just a minute, Mrs. Wiggins. Where are you taking those children? I understood they have an uncle out west."

A look of contempt flashed in Mrs. Wiggins's eyes. "Them lumberjacks! They'd be late fer their own funerals, so they would. He's a comin' for them in two weeks, or so he says."

"And why...I mean...did their mother ask *you* to care for them till then?"

"Ask? She couldn't hardly breathe, let alone talk! No, she didn't leave no instructions at all. Their Uncle Willy's only takin' 'em cause he's their next of kin. There's no one else left related to 'em."

It was on the tip of Marilla's tongue to point out that *she* was left—after all, a third cousin is also a blood relative. But the doubts with which she had wrestled ever since her last visit to Mary's sickbed silenced her.

"If ever you need help in any way, Mrs. Wiggins, you'll find me at Green Gables, over in Avonlea." It was all she could manage to offer.

"Thank you right kindly, Miss Cuthbert," replied Mrs. Wiggins. "I raised five of my own, so I figger I c'n manage these two for two weeks. It's the least I can do as a Christian neighbor." The harsh lines on her face softened for a moment. "I was awful fond of their poor Ma." With that, she marched off to her wagon, hauling the two children after her.

"Ouch!" yelled Davy, stumbling in his heavy shoes. "Don't yank. I don't like yanking."

"The louder you yells, the harder I yanks," replied Mrs. Wiggins, giving both arms an extra yank for good measure.

Marilla stared after them. With all her heart she longed to call them back. But something held her silent. What was it—fear, caution, a sense of her own inadequacy? She had no answer. Turning, she stared down into the grave. Already the gravediggers had begun shoveling earth on the wooden casket. "Goodbye, Mary," she whispered. "God rest your soul." Raising her hand, she dropped the bouquet of wildflowers she carried onto the coffin. She had risen especially early that morning to pick them, knowing they were Mary's favorites. She had made that small gesture, but she was unable to make the larger, more important one. If Mary were to show herself now, Marilla knew she would not be able to look her in the eye. Ashamed and disquieted, she turned away.

Chapter Four

While Marilla had been busy with the children, Rachel had not remained idle. Naturally she had felt rebuffed when Marilla hurried over to the grave, completely ignoring her. She had stood there, holding her aching jaw and wishing she had just not bothered to come. After all, Mary Keith was Marilla's relative, not hers. Nobody in Rachel's family had ever had the bad taste to die young. Every single one had lived a life of exasperatingly good health and had popped off only when they were good and ready.

Still, it would serve Marilla right if Rachel were to prove the exception to the rule. Marilla had taken her for granted far too long. Why, only this morning, instead of consoling her friend for being in pain, Marilla had snapped at her to get a move on. No, Rachel thought darkly, dying had certain attractions, not the least of which was the way people sympathized with you. Take Mary Keith, now. If she hadn't gone and died, nobody would have paid the least bit of attention to her. Of course, if she, Rachel, were to die, she felt sure she could manage it with a bit more flair than poor Mary. Not that there was anything morally wrong with pine coffins, apart, of course, from their discomfort. But once one has the attention of the community, why not display a little more, well, ostentation. Perhaps dignity was a better word. Dignity and style— that's what dying was all about.

Rachel raised her head and looked about with a clearer eye. The pain in her tooth had abated somewhat. She felt resolved, refreshed. Yes, there was a lot to be said for dying well.

At that moment, a man standing at the back of the funeral crowd detached himself and approached Mrs. Lynde. Rachel saw him coming. She watched as he worked his way through the crowd, murmuring an apology here, doffing his hat there. Another important word popped into her head: distinguished. Never, in all her life, had she seen anyone so downright distinguished as this black-suited gentleman. Well, almost never.

She adjusted her hat and waited.

"Forgive the intrusion, Madam. Are you perchance a relative of the deceased?"

He was standing right in front of her. He had removed his hat, revealing oily strands of dark hair pasted firmly across an ivory scalp. His long, thin face was pale, his eyes a light, almost colorless, blue.

Rachel did something she had not done in years. She blushed. She couldn't recall the last time a distinguished gentleman had addressed her in such hushed, almost reverent tones. Forgetting all about her toothache and Marilla's impatience, she smiled warmly.

"Not a relative, no. But I'm the close friend of a relative, Miss Cuthbert. That's her, over there, talking to those bratty looking children."

He did not remove his pale eyes from her face. Extending a gloved hand, he reached for hers.

"Mr. Silas Drabble, undertaker by profession, at your service, Madam."

"Pleased to make your acquaintance, Mr. Babble," babbled Rachel, hoping Marilla could see her talking to this eminent-looking personage. "My name is Rachel Lynde, widow of Thomas Lynde." And is there, she wanted to ask, a Mrs. Babble?

"Drabble," he corrected, with a mournful smile. "I trust yours is not a recent loss?"

"Oh no," replied Rachel cheerfully, "my Thomas died several years ago. I've been living with Miss Cuthbert at Green Gables ever since."

This time Silas Drabble allowed his eyes to leave Rachel's face and follow in the direction she indicated. They gleamed as they caught sight of Marilla, dignified in her best black muslin.

"Ah," he sighed, "another lady of respectable vintage."

Rachel nodded agreeably, not quite catching his drift.

"In this uncertain world, Madam, the only certainty is death."

"Amen to that," sighed Rachel devoutly.

"And when one reaches one's mature years, one really should plan for that ultimate certainty, don't you agree?"

"Of course, Mr. Bibble, I mean, Bobble." Rachel was so busy studying the form, she had not quite absorbed the content.

"Er, Drabble, Mrs. Lynde, Silas Drabble." A white card, trimmed with black, had appeared in Mr. Drabble's gloved hand. He held it out to Rachel. "I represent the Lasting Memorial Casket Company, Mrs. Lynde. We provide a complete service: casket, stone, epitaph. Always tasteful, always reasonable. God willing, you and your friend have many productive years ahead of you still, but should 'death's winged chariot' draw near, hail me first."

Rachel stared at him. Was this man heaven-sent? Just minutes ago she had been giving serious consideration to her own funeral, and now here he was, an expert, qualified to advise on the most stylish way to meet one's Maker. It was with difficulty that she restrained herself from clasping him to her bosom.

"Why, Mr. Dribble," Rachel gushed. "How very fortunate you should happen by. I've always said, if you're going to do something, do it thoroughly. I am noted for that. And I have no intention of shirking my own death." Seizing his card, she studied it greedily.

Behind her, an elderly man, led by his middle-aged son, tottered into view. Along with most of the mourners, they had left the graveside and were heading back towards the buggies, the service now at an end. Mr. Drabble craned his long, thin neck, studying the pair with a practiced eye. Prime material there, no doubt about it. Carefully replacing his hat, he bowed towards Mrs. Lynde. His lips parted in the ghost of a smile.

Rachel caught a glimpse of impeccably polished, marble-white teeth. Like well-kept tombstones, she thought enviously. Mindful of her own decaying monuments, she smiled back, keeping her mouth carefully closed.

"Goodbye, Mrs. Lynde. And remember, death is what you make of it."

Rachel positively glowed. "My feelings exactly, Mr. Piddle. In fact, that's always been my motto. If a thing's worth doing, it's worth doing w—"

But Mr. Drabble, unaccountably, did not stay to hear Rachel's motto. He hurried off through the crowd, on the trail of the most likely-looking candidate for his custom-made coffins.

Chapter Five

"I'm going downhill fast, I can tell. The pain's something terrible. Ooohh!"

For the twelfth time that afternoon, Rachel groaned aloud. Out of the corner of her eye, she glanced over at Marilla, but Marilla's attention seemed fixed on her second cup of tea.

"I tell you, this mouth of mine's so swollen it makes me feel like a chipmunk," persisted Rachel. "There's no doubt about it, Marilla. Once swelling sets into a tooth, you might as well give up the ghost. A body's as good as dead."

"Nobody ever died of a toothache, Rachel. How many times do I have to tell you? If it's aching so much, go see Dr. Blair and have it pulled."

"Pulled? Are you out of your mind? Why, there's only so much pain a body can stand! Besides, the McNabs and the Lyndes have all died with a full set of teeth, and so will I—very shortly, if I'm not mistaken. But *I* intend to go prepared. Unlike some I could mention."

Not the faintest flicker of interest animated Marilla's face. She continued sipping her tea, determined not to rise to Rachel's bait.

Rachel picked up the black-rimmed card lying on the table beside her and studied it ostentatiously. Only two days had elapsed since Mary Keith's funeral, but already Rachel had written to Mr. Drabble about her own death. She had skimmed discreetly over the cause of her imminent demise. To admit to mortally rotten teeth to a man endowed with a full and healthy set was, she felt, unbearably humiliating. She had merely mentioned a mysterious disease that was about to strike her down in her prime. Then she had moved bravely on to discuss the effect she wished to produce at her own funeral. The look of the casket, she had stressed, was all-important. What she wanted was something prestigious, something streamlined, a fitting receptacle for a person of her position in the community. Only towards the end had she ventured to inquire about costs.

"I wonder how much oak would set me back?" she murmured now, peering at the card as though the price of each casket were inscribed there in invisible ink.

The words jumped from Marilla before she could stop them. "Tear up that card, for heaven's sake, Rachel. You don't need a casket."

"I certainly don't need a plain pine one, thank you very much. What comfort poor Mary could get out of a wretched little box like that is beyond me. It looked naked as a jaybird, so it did, without so much as one teensy-weensy brass ornament, or even a hinge."

Marilla raised her eyes to heaven. If Rachel didn't stop harping on that same old string, she would scream. The sound of a carriage drawing to a stop outside the house promised some relief. Looking out the window, she was thankful to see Sara and Olivia dismounting from their buggy.

"Who is it?" demanded Rachel, retreating behind the living-room door. Ever since her jaw had swollen up, she had taken to avoiding windows. She had no desire to be seen looking as though a croquet ball had lodged in her cheek.

"It's only Sara and Olivia. They've come to take a photograph of you."

"Photograph of me? In my condition? What on earth for? Don't tell me the toothache is all that unusual?"

"It's nothing to do with your toothache, Rachel. It's about the church choir. I told them you were the one who got it started."

"Why, of course I did. If it hadn't been for my get up and go—"

Rachel stopped short, vanity vying with vanity. She certainly wanted the world to know about her role in starting the church choir. On the other hand, did she really want the world to see her with her cheek puffed out like a toad's? After a moment's reflection, she came down firmly on the side of glory-at-all-costs. Credit where credit is due, she decided. Besides, she could always turn her swollen cheek away from the camera. Glancing down at her dress, she gave a yelp of distress.

"Don't let them in, Marilla. I haven't even got my corset on!"

"Then go upstairs and *put* your corset on!"

"You should have been a general, Marilla Cuthbert! All you do is order people about!" Picking up her skirts, Rachel fled upstairs before her exasperated friend could open the front door.

Marilla welcomed Sara and Olivia warmly. What with Rachel's constant talk of death and caskets, and her own private anxiety over poor Mary, she was happy to accommodate any distraction. That morning, while listening to Rachel's litany of aches and pains, she had baked one of her legendary blueberry pies. This she now pressed on her two guests.

Sara accepted gratefully, but Olivia declined. Olivia had not been working at the Avonlea *Chronicle* long enough to feel completely confident in her new role as newspaperwoman. Normally she would have been accompanied on her rounds by Jasper Dale, Avonlea's resident genius and the owner of a fine, temperamental camera. While Olivia asked questions and wrote down the answers, Jasper would handle the photographs. Shy and retiring as he was, Jasper always managed, somehow, to inspire confidence in Olivia. Unfortunately, he had been called away to Charlottetown on business, and today Olivia was feeling his absence keenly. She was not quite sure she could manage the camera on her own. It seemed to require so much adjusting and coaxing and all-round attention that she could not help thinking of it as an oversized, unpredictable lap-dog, which might at any moment yelp loudly and piddle on the carpet. She had taken her niece along as her assistant, but for the moment Sara seemed far more interested in blueberry pie than in helping. Trying not to panic, Olivia positioned the camera in the corner by the piano. She had decided to photograph Mrs. Lynde with her hands poised over the keys.

Sara had blissfully gulped down two slices of pie before she realized that Olivia had set up the camera and was now trying to coax the leafy aspidistra to wave gracefully in the background. Clearly it was high time she made herself useful.

"I hear Mrs. Lynde will be singing at the church picnic this year," Sara began, setting down her fork reluctantly. "Has she always been a singer?"

"For as long as I've known her," replied Marilla, her pride in her friend coming to the fore. "Rachel had a lovely voice as a young girl. She was in great demand as a soloist, and for duets, too."

"Did she ever sing a duet with anyone famous?"

"Not with anyone outside the Island. Although there was a fairly well-known young minister with a fine tenor voice. He had his own choir...."

Marilla's voice trailed off. A guarded look crept into her face. Oh dear, a sensitive area. She had better tread carefully. Perhaps she had already gone too far?

"Anyone we might have heard of, Miss Cuthbert?" persisted Sara.

"No, no. I don't think so. Besides, Rachel married Thomas shortly afterwards. She had more important things to do then than sing."

Sara inhaled deeply. The romantic implications were inescapable.

"You mean Mrs. Lynde abandoned her talent when she found true love?"

"Well, not exactly...."

Marilla felt trapped. How on earth had she managed to get herself embroiled in such a delicate matter? She cast desperately around for a change of topic. A querulous call from Rachel rescued her in the nick of time.

"Can you please come up here, Marilla? I need your help." The voice sounded muffled and scratchy. Excusing herself, Marilla hurried towards the stairs.

"Miss Cuthbert? You don't happen to have any choir memorabilia, do you? Programs, or perhaps a photograph of Mrs. Lynde from that time?"

Another whine floated downstairs. "Where are you, Marilla? I can't, for the life of me, find my you-know-what!"

"Oh yes, Miss Cuthbert." Olivia added her appeal to Sara's. "You know what they say in the newspaper business, 'One picture is worth a thousand words.'"

Marilla paused, her hand on the newel. She felt flustered and out of her depth. "Rachel did put some of her old papers in the storeroom," she answered doubtfully. "Although I'm not sure she'd want people looking through her personal belongings."

"Oh, we won't look at anything personal, Miss Cuthbert," Olivia assured her. "We're only interested in old choir papers, the types of hymns people favored then, that sort of thing. And pictures, of course."

"Marilla! I'll thank you to come if you're coming! I need you *now*, not tomorrow night!"

"Very well, ladies. You may take a look in the storeroom. But I would ask you to remember two things. First, when Mrs. Lynde comes downstairs, please do not mention her swollen face. She's had a toothache for a week now and she's awful testy. She's convinced she's at death's door." Marilla placed her foot on the bottom stair. "Just simmer down, Rachel. I'm coming!"

"Miss Cuthbert?"

She turned, halfway up the stairs. "Yes, Olivia?"

"What's the second thing?"

"Second thing?"

"The second thing you want us to remember?"

"Of course. How silly of me. The second thing." Marilla struggled to find the right way to phrase it. "Please...my dears...please do not pry into old stories best forgotten."

With these mysterious words, Marilla turned and disappeared upstairs.

Chapter Six

Tiptoeing into the storeroom, Sara and Olivia intended merely to search for old photographs, battered hymnals or sheet music tucked away on dusty shelves. They certainly did not mean to pry. The hope chest was the first object to meet their gaze. It stood there brazenly, seeming to court their attention. Carved on its lid were the initials "R. McN."

"Of course, Rachel McNab!" whispered Olivia. "That was her name before she married Thomas Lynde."

Without stopping to think, they raised the lid. On top of old letters, tied neatly in colored ribbons, lay a framed photograph. Sara pulled it out.

"This must have been Rachel when she was young. My goodness, how lovely she was!"

For some reason, the sight of Mrs. Lynde as a pretty young girl surprised Sara beyond all expectation. Imaginative though she was, she found it difficult to believe that anyone middle-aged had ever been as young and slim as herself. If the truth were known, she found the idea frightening, too. For if dumpy Mrs.

Lynde, with her gray hair, jowly neck and loud voice had once looked like Sara, then what were Sara's prospects when she herself arrived at Mrs. Lynde's age? The thought did not bear scrutiny.

"Let me see," urged Olivia, reaching for the faded photograph. As she took it from Sara, the old wooden frame, already loose, came apart in her hands. Between its front and back, another small photograph was visible.

Sara tugged at it gently. "My, oh my!" she gasped. "This must have been Thomas! You never told me he was so handsome, Aunt Olivia."

"He wasn't," replied Olivia, wrinkling up her nose as she tried to remember. "Not the Thomas Lynde I knew. He was a small, homely man with mousy hair and a heart of gold."

"This man's dark, and he's tall, and he's, well, he's simply devastatingly handsome." Sara tore her eyes away from the face in the photograph and handed it to Olivia.

"That's not Thomas," said Olivia slowly. "Poor Thomas never looked like that. Not once in his whole life." She turned the picture over. A lock of lustrous, jet-black hair had been affixed to the back with glue and a narrow blue ribbon. The inscription was faded, but still legible. "To my Rachel," it read. "She walks in beauty like the night..." It was signed simply: "A. D."

Their eyes moved, as though hypnotized, from the

picture of a radiant, girlish Rachel to that of the dashing young man. He looked, Sara thought, wonderfully distinguished and almost wickedly handsome. Long, dark lashes framed the black, mocking eyes. The full, perfect mouth seemed about to tilt upwards into a smile of conspiracy. He was dressed formally in a dark suit with a high, stiff collar. A gold watch chain hung between two pockets. He might have been a famous young tenor on his first world tour. He might have been a Greek god disguised in human clothing. But under no circumstances might he have been Thomas Lynde. Of this Sara was now convinced.

"Look at this!" Olivia had been rummaging in the hope chest. Mindful of Marilla's warning, she had avoided touching any letters. But books, surely books were safe to examine? Now she held out a leather-bound songbook, which she had found tucked into a corner of the chest. Stamped on the flyleaf were the words "The Touring Evangelical Choir." The pages were edged in gold and very brittle. She turned them over carefully. Then she stopped. On the fourth page, opposite "Love Divine, all loves excelling," lay a dried red rose. Attached to it was a small card on which were penned the letters "A. D." Around them someone had drawn a perfect heart.

Olivia and Sara gazed at each other in amazement. "A hidden photograph, a handsome young man, a loving dedication, a heart with the initials

A.D. and a dried rose," itemized Sara. "My goodness, Aunt Olivia. It all adds up to an intriguing mystery, doesn't it? It seems there's more to Mrs. Lynde than meets the eye."

Olivia looked troubled. "Marilla did warn us not to pry into stories best forgotten. But, oh Sara, how can we possibly ignore a story like this?"

Upstairs, unaware of the momentous discoveries being made in her storeroom, Marilla struggled to lever Rachel into her corset. Her corpulent friend managed to make a difficult exercise well-nigh impossible by fidgeting incessantly.

"Get a move on, Marilla," she fussed, fiddling with her hair. "I can't keep my public waiting forever."

"Keep still and suck in that stomach!"

The corset extended from Rachel's bust to below her hips and was lined with whalebone. It laced up the back, producing, when firmly tied, a sleek, hourglass figure. Some figures are more compliant than others, however, and forcing Rachel's exuberant flesh into a conventional straitjacket was an exhausting process. While Rachel anchored herself to the bed by locking both hands around the bedpost, Marilla stood behind her, heaving with all her strength on the laces, which she tied into a series of knots, one below the other.

"Ouch! You caught a bit of skin! Can't you be more careful?"

"That's not skin, it's pure blubber," replied Marilla

through clenched teeth, hauling at a particularly stubborn lace.

Rachel had been holding her breath, trying to flatten her stomach. Now she expelled it all in a rush, popping the lace which Marilla had only just managed to tie.

"Are you suggesting I'm fat, Marilla Cuthbert?"

"I asked you not to breathe, Rachel!" exploded Marilla. "And I'm not suggesting, I'm telling you. You think a mite too much of your insides for your own good. It's getting harder and harder to force you into this contraption."

"Twaddle! My figure's the same as it was twenty years ago. It's your eyesight that's changed, Marilla. You're having trouble fitting them laces into them little holes, only you're too vain to admit it. Why, you can't see the nose in front of your face anymore. Don't think I haven't noticed, because I have. You've been squinting. And what's worse, you've been pretending not to!"

Marilla opened her mouth, intending to shout even louder than Rachel. On second thought, she shut it again. Giving a final yank at the last lace, she wrenched it into a knot and marched downstairs, leaving Rachel to finish dressing alone. There was no point getting into a shouting match with Rachel Lynde. Her lungs were far stronger than Marilla's. No, Marilla decided, she had enough worries to deal with for the moment. She would bide her time, and if the situation with Rachel did not improve, then she would have to think about asking her to look for somewhere else to live at the end of the month.

To Olivia's relief, the photographic session took place without mishap. Although Rachel seemed to be having some difficulty breathing, her smile remained gracious. Sitting at the keyboard, she willingly adopted several different poses, only insisting that it be her right profile she lifted to the lens and not her left. Questioned about her role in starting Avonlea's first choir, she replied with great volubility and could only be silenced by the sight of the last slice of blueberry pie being offered to Sara. Sara, feeling Mrs. Lynde's eye upon her, dutifully declined.

As Rachel, quiet at last, tucked into the last piece of pie, Olivia asked her final question.

"You never mentioned the Touring Evangelical Choir, Mrs. Lynde. It sounds as though it might make an interesting subject for an article. Can you tell me, for instance, about someone who might have been involved in the choir? His initials were A.D."

Rachel raised her head, clasping at her throat. A choking sound emerged. Perhaps crumbs had lodged in her windpipe, perhaps a whole blueberry? Her eyes watered, and she coughed uncontrollably. Marilla rushed to fetch a glass of water. Rachel took it without a word and drank it down slowly. The coughing ceased. She seemed to be playing for time. But Sara could wait no longer. Unbeknownst to Olivia, Sara had taken the photograph of the young man from Rachel's hope chest, and now, bursting with curiousity, she held it up to Rachel.

"What about him, Mrs. Lynde?" she asked, "Were they *his* initials?"

Rachel looked as though she were about to burst a blood vessel. Snatching the photograph from Sara she jumped to her feet. "How *dare* you?" she gasped. She glared at Marilla, her breath coming in short gasps. "Marilla Cuthbert!" she stormed. "How *could* you let them snoop in my private papers?!"

Marilla looked chagrined. "I had no idea that you had kept his picture, Rachel. Otherwise I would never have allowed—"

"Well I did. And you did. And heaven only knows what kind of dog's dinner you've landed us in now!"

Olivia looked over at Sara, her eyes sounding the retreat. As quietly as they could, they gathered up their equipment and edged towards the hall.

"We'll let ourselves out, Miss Cuthbert, Mrs. Lynde," ventured Olivia. "Thank you both for your hospitality."

Pulling herself together, Marilla followed them to the front door and closed it behind them. As she turned back into the room, she saw a fat tear slide from Rachel's eye and roll down her cheek.

"What's a body to do, Marilla?" she moaned. "My tooth feels like there's hornets making merry in it, them girls won't rest till they've found out about Ambrose and me, and my liver feels like it's been shoved clean into my stomach."

Marilla put her arm around Rachel's shoulder. "Come upstairs and I'll help you off with that corset, Rachel," she said gently. "Then I think you should ask Dr. Blair to have a look at your tooth."

Chapter Seven

Hetty King laid down her feather duster and eyed her youngest sister thoughtfully. "The Touring Evangelical Choir?" she repeated. "Now what in the world would you want to know about that for?"

Olivia scratched her head with her pencil. "You mean you know about it? I've lived all my life in Avonlea and I've never heard of any touring evangelical singers."

"Proof once again, Olivia, that you don't know everything."

"Well, why did you never mention them before?"

"You never asked."

Olivia tried to keep the exasperation out of her

voice. "I'm asking now, Hetty? Who were they?"

Hetty traced a decorative pattern with the duster along the edge of the sofa. She seemed to be thinking hard.

"Well, they were a group of young singers, don't you know?"

"I had gathered that much, Hetty."

"They used to visit Avonlea regularly. They were...quite...popular. What else do you need to know?"

"Simply everything. Did they have a leader, a conductor?"

Hetty lifted a piece of fluff from the sofa and gazed at it thoughtfully. "Why, yes, I believe they did."

"His name, Hetty. What was his name?"

"His name." Hetty studied the piece of fluff, as though it might possibly contain a written list of names. Her voice was offhand, almost careless. "It wasn't an everyday name, don't you know? In fact, it would be hard to forget a name like that."

"What was it?"

Hetty's hand lifted to her hair, smoothing it in place. She smiled, a fond, girlish smile. The years seemed to drop away from her. She appeared to have completely forgotten about Olivia and Sara.

"I remember thinking how perfectly his name suited him, because he was handsome as a god, a Greek god. And all the ladies buzzed after him, as ladies will, like bees to a honey pot. Nectar of the gods...ambrosia...yes,

Ambrose Dinsdale certainly lived up to his name."

"A.D.!" exclaimed Sara, who had been sitting quietly on a chair in the study until now, observing her Aunt Hetty. "Oh, I just wish Rachel hadn't snatched that photograph away! We could have shown it to you for confirmation."

"Rachel Lynde has kept a photograph of Ambrose Dinsdale?" Aunt Hetty seemed to waken from a dream. "Rachel Lynde! Why, mercy me! And she a married woman!" Hetty had turned white. There was a moment's silence as she stood there, twisting the duster in her fingers. "I had no idea he knew her all that well," she murmured. "Well enough to give her a photograph." She glared at Olivia. "What did she tell you about him?"

"Nothing at all. She just went red as a beet when we asked her about the initials A.D. and showed her the photograph."

"I think it spoilt the blueberry pie for her well and truly," said Sara gloomily. "What a shameful waste. She might as well have let me have it."

"Did she tell you they sang duets together? Not often, mind you. Only once. Twice at the most."

"No, she never mentioned duets. Although Marilla did say something about them. Poor Marilla!" exclaimed Olivia. "Rachel really gave her the sharp side of her tongue when she found out that Marilla let us into the storeroom."

"How Marilla Cuthbert puts up with that woman is beyond me." Hetty resumed her dusting. The brightly colored feathers flicked the heavy volumes that lined the shelves. She had stopped humming, Sara noticed. Nor did she run her fingers along the top edge and down the spine of certain books, as was her wont. Sara had often watched her before and knew this gesture had as much to do with enjoying the feel of the books themselves as it did with checking for any remaining traces of dust.

Now Hetty's mind seemed busy elsewhere. She snapped when Olivia asked if she had known Mr. Dinsdale.

"Of course not—I mean—who knows anybody, really? Ambro—I mean, Mr. Dinsdale was a charming man, with excellent manners. And I, well *I* certainly wasn't married..." Her voice trailed off.

Olivia stared at her sister. "Rachel probably wasn't married either, Hetty. She was very young at that time. And very pretty."

"I was just as pretty as she was. Prettier, some said!" Hetty put a hand to her lips, trying to quell an emotion she had thought long buried.

"Why, of course you were, Hetty. You were pretty as a picture."

Sara looked closely at her Aunt Hetty. What on earth was the matter with her? The hand holding the duster shook slightly. A look of bitterness had come

over her face. It was hard to believe she had once
been as pretty as Olivia said.

"Was Mr. Dinsdale a good singer, Aunt Hetty?"
she asked suddenly.

The bitterness faded out of Hetty's eyes. "He
sang like an angel, Sara. I don't think I've ever heard
a sweeter voice. Not before. Not since. Listening to
him, you could forget you were an earthbound crea-
ture. He seemed to lift you out of yourself, upwards.
He made you forget you were mortal."

Aunt Hetty's eyes filled with tears. She turned
back to the bookshelves and blindly resumed her
dusting. Olivia, checking over her notes, seemed
unaware of her sister's odd behavior.

"You know what I think, Hetty?" she said thoughtfully. "I think I should write an article about the Touring Evangelical Choir. After all, it seems to have
played quite an important part in people's lives."

"You might say that, Olivia," came Hetty's stran-
gled reply.

"Very well, then." Olivia snapped her notebook
shut. "I'll get started on the research. Would you like
to help me, Sara?"

Sara nodded, one eye on her elder aunt. "Would
that be all right, Aunt Hetty?"

"Why wouldn't it be?" snapped Hetty, without
turning around. "No newspaperwoman worth her
salt is going to stop investigating a story she considers

worthwhile. Especially," she muttered acidly, "if it has a strong element of human interest."

"Come along then, Sara!" Olivia hurried out of the room.

Sara glanced back at Aunt Hetty. She was standing quite still, facing her books. The feather duster hung limp in one hand. As though finally aware of Sara's gaze, she turned.

"Let me know," she said bleakly. "Let me know what you find out."

Chapter Eight

There it was again—a snuffling, gobbling noise. Rachel banged her pen down on the kitchen table and stood up crossly. She was in the throes of composing another letter to her undertaker. Composition was not good for Rachel's soul. It made her anxious and irritable, adding to the general feeling of tension caused by her toothache. By now her jaw was so swollen that she had wrapped a bandage around it, tying it clumsily at the top of her head so that she looked like a huge, mechanical wind-up toy.

"If that's that Harrison pig sniffing at my flowers, I'll make bacon of it for breakfast!" The Harrison's pig was known for its forays into other people's gardens.

Rachel and the pig had long been engaged in mortal combat.

"I thought you weren't ever going to eat again with that pain in your tooth," remarked Marilla, who was rolling out dough for a meat pie.

"No need to remind me of my fleshly limitations, Marilla, but you can be sure of one thing. If the pain doesn't kill me, starvation will. I swear, not a crumb's crossed my lips since this tooth started to ache."

Marilla held tightly to her rolling pin. If Rachel chose to believe she was capable of starving to death, it was not in Marilla's power to disillusion her. "Sit down and finish your letter, Rachel, and stop moaning on about dying," was all she said.

"I'll moan on about dying as long as I'm alive, Marilla. And while I'm alive I do not intend to let that revolting porker ruin my gladioli!" Grabbing her apron to flap at the offending animal, Rachel hurried out of the kitchen and onto the veranda.

With a sigh, Marilla sat down at the table and closed her eyes. Any minute now, Rachel would raise her voice and utter the unearthly shriek she reserved for the Harrison's pig. It was a shriek that never failed to slice into Marilla's temples like a cleaver. But just as Marilla raised her floury hands to cover her ears, she heard Rachel gasp as though gulping back a shriek. Her voice sounded soft and ingratiating and totally unlike her usual squawk. "Why, good morning,

Mr. Squabble," she heard Rachel say. "What a pleasant surprise. I was expecting a pig."

A man's voice answered, an unctuous, sticky bass. It reminded Marilla of treacle spreading in a slow pool across a scrubbed floor. "Good morning, Mrs. Lynde," oozed the voice. " I've come to measure you for your casket."

Marilla pushed back her chair and walked out to the veranda. A man stood by the door, hat in hand. His face vied with his shirt for whiteness. His suit was black as night. In all her life, Marilla had never seen such colorless eyes. They reminded her of highly polished windows. On seeing Marilla, a light seemed to flash on in them. Quickly returning his hat to his head, he removed it again with a flourish. "Silas Drabble, at your service, Madam," he bowed. "Allow me to wish you a very good morning."

Marilla returned his bow stiffly. Something about the man set her teeth on edge. Yet Rachel seemed blithely unconscious of his unsavory aspect. All her crossness had evaporated. Her swollen face was wreathed in smiles. "Step right in, Mr. Rabble!" she gushed. "I'm powerful glad to see you. You've saved me putting pen to paper a second time!"

Beneath the veranda, in plain view of all, the Harrisons' pig had clamped his jaws firmly around Rachel's prize gladioli and was digging his hind legs deeper into the soil, the better to get a purchase on the defenseless plants. Yet Rachel seemed oblivious to the havoc being wrought under her very nose. She had eyes only for her undertaker. Opening the screen door, she ushered him inside. Marilla had no choice but to stand back and let him enter.

"Let's get down to business straight away," she heard Rachel say, as she waved him into the front parlor and settled her plump posterior in Marilla's favorite chair. "Departing in style takes planning. Planning takes time, and believe me, I've none to waste."

"Indeed, dear lady. In my line of work, one never knows if one may be too late," replied Mr. Drabble. "That is why, rather than reply by letter, I took the liberty of calling in person."

"That was most thoughtful of you. Please make yourself at home. Take off your things. Marilla will fetch you a cup of tea."

Marilla snorted. She had no intention of offering Mr. Drabble the time of day, let alone a cup of tea.

Mr. Drabble was not to be diverted from his mission, however. "Business before pleasure, Mrs. Lynde," he murmured, removing a large measuring tape from his gladstone bag. "Business before pleasure. Now, if you would just stand for me." He waved the tape at her encouragingly. Rachel jumped to her feet and submitted herself enthusiastically to be measured. It pleased her to see the care with which Mr. Drabble wrote down her generous dimensions in a

black notebook, having first licked his stubby pencil
with the palest of tongues.

"And don't forget to do Marilla, too," she urged,
as soon as he had finished, fearful lest her friend feel
left out.

Mr. Drabble eyed Marilla cautiously. Miss Cuthbert, although of suitable age, did not seem in the
least inclined to be measured for a casket. As though
to confirm this suspicion, Marilla had turned her
back on the intruder and was doing her best to
ignore him. Approaching from behind, Mr. Drabble
held the tape out gingerly. He looked like an anxious
dog-catcher about to collar an unreliable mongrel.

"Come along now, Miss Cuthbert," he urged.
"This won't hurt a bit. All I need is your height and
width."

Marilla turned, drew herself up to her full height
and eyed Mr. Drabble frostily from head to foot.

"Oh go on, Marilla." Rachel adopted her most
cajoling tone. "Poor Mr. Bubble travelled all the way
from Carmody just to measure us. You're not going
to let him go home empty-handed, are you?"

"Of course she's not. Of course she's not," soothed
Mr. Drabble. Arms outstretched, he tiptoed forward
and attempted to place his tape around Marilla's
waist. But Marilla was having none of that. Lifting
one hand, she caught the tape and wrapped it deftly
around Mr. Drabble's bony wrists.

"I'll thank you to keep your implements to yourself, sir," she snapped. "I refuse to be measured for a casket and that is final."

His arms locked together, Mr. Drabble tottered backwards into an armchair, where he proceeded to unwrap himself in safety.

Rachel shook her head disapprovingly. How *could* Marilla treat a distinguished guest with such rudeness? Yet she knew better than to confront her friend once her temper was up. Instead, she tried another tack.

"Now Marilla," she reasoned. "You know how you dislike wasting money. Let's face it, sooner or later we're both going to need caskets, so why not buy two together and save a pretty penny?"

"I am not ready to die yet, Rachel Lynde, and neither are you."

Having worked his hands free, Mr. Drabble drew his cavernous bag onto his knees and scrabbled in its depths. "When you *are* ready to die, Madam," he panted, drawing out a booklet and waving it in Marilla's direction, "I have the perfect setting for you. It's our number fifty-three. The pride of our company: pure oak, hand-carved." His pale eyes gleamed softly. "Fifty cents a month for five years or until your demise, whichever comes first."

"Well now," ventured Rachel. "That's a mighty good price for solid oak. Wouldn't you agree, Marilla?

Decked out in that, it's not likely you'd feel ashamed at your own funeral."

Marilla did not deign to reply. Taking her silence for encouragement, Mr. Drabble pressed on. "We carry only the very finest of satin linings." His voice was hushed, reverential. "All in splendid but subtle colors. Buttercup yellow, peacock blue, palest pink or..." He paused for effect. "...our very latest—mauve."

"Mauve is really *my* color," interrupted Rachel jealously. She was not sure what color mauve was, but she felt Marilla was occupying rather more of the undertaker's attention than she deserved. "So please make a note of that, Mr. Scrabble. Now, as for my laying out. I've planned it all in some detail. I shall be attired in my watered silk with the pearl buttons and my best lace shawl. I've polished my new shoes. You'll find them at the back of my cupboard wrapped in a red flannel cloth. As for crimping, I refuse to let anyone crimp my hair. I cannot abide crimping on a corpse. Where's that pencil of yours, Mr. Scribble? Shouldn't you be taking notes? Then there's the question of horses. I think six horses pulling my carriage would be an appropriate number. What do you think, Marilla?"

"Rachel Lynde, have you taken leave of your senses? There you sit, planning your funeral down to the last detail, when all you have to do is ask Dr. Blair to yank that tooth out of your fool head and let us all get on with our lives!"

"Now Marilla, there's no good letting the green-eyed monster get the best of you. Just because I thought of dying first. Mr. Rabble here offered to take your measurements too. Marilla?! Come back here! Now what on earth's gotten into that woman?"

Marilla had suddenly turned and rushed out of the room. Rachel flashed an embarrassed smile at the undertaker. "Please pay her no attention, Mr. Grovel. She's just not used to getting buried. Besides, she's been acting strange ever since poor Mary Keith was took poorly."

Mr. Drabble lowered his glassy eyes in understanding. "Death is never easy, dear lady," he sighed. "But it is *certainly* more comfortable in solid oak."

"Amen to that," nodded Rachel. Neither of them knew quite what to say next.

In the silence that followed, they heard Marilla's voice speaking with apparent calm. "Welcome, Mrs. Wiggins," she was saying. "How nice of you to bring the children for a visit."

Chapter Nine

Rachel was right about one thing: from the moment Marilla had heard of Mary's illness, she had not known a moment's peace of mind. It had come to her clearly that henceforth her life and the lives of

Mary's children would be inextricably bound. She had grasped this fully and intuitively, yet she refused to allow her mind to dwell on it. She could not bring herself to make plans, or to discuss the situation with Rachel or anyone else. In the absence of more tangible evidence—legal arguments, documentary proof, a word from Mary—she had tried to behave as though nothing were demanded of her.

Even now, with the two children staring up at her and Mrs. Wiggins roaring in her ear, she could not bring herself to acknowledge that this visit was anything more than a brief social call.

This is not to say that Marilla was hard-hearted. Brought up to weigh every decision in the scales of reason and logic, she had learned from an early age to be suspicious of anything she could not turn over in her hands and measure. Impulse, instinct, intuition—these words had no place in Marilla's lexicon, yet they formed a major part of her character. Thus, for weeks now, one half of her conscience had been at war with the other. Instinct pointed to the children and their need. Upbringing wrestled with instinct, arguing instead that no one had asked her to intervene, that she was merely a distant relative, that she was old, that she had little money, that she already had Rachel Lynde living at Green Gables. Small wonder that she felt worn out. Small wonder that Rachel's noisy obsession with caskets was driving her to distraction. Marilla's heart and mind were tearing her in two, and until one was reconciled with the other, she would have no rest.

She had not been in the least surprised to see Mrs. Wiggins arrive with the children, yet she could not just hold out her arms, as her heart bade her, and welcome them unreservedly. No, she must keep a pretence of distance. By all means thank Mrs. Wiggins for coming. But at the same time make it plain that neither she nor the children were expected to stay.

Mrs. Wiggins was not interested in Marilla's crisis of conscience. She wanted release. "I won't tolerate another minute of this boy!" she was screaming at Marilla. "He's et me out of house and home. He's broke my best platter. An' this morning he yanked the feathers out of my prize rooster!"

Davy squirmed uncomfortably in Mrs. Wiggins's grasp. In one hand he held a battered valise, in the other his pet frog. Marilla tried not to look at him. At any moment, she feared, her defenses might crumble.

"I'm sorry to hear he hasn't been behaving, Mrs. Wiggins," she replied politely. "What would you like me to do about it?"

"Do about it? Do about it? I don't give two cents what you do about it. I'm through with him, that's all. You can hold onto him till his Uncle Willy comes. Or you can feed him to the pigs. I wash my hands of him altogether."

So saying, she released her hold on Davy's collar so suddenly that he fell to the ground. Dora immediately set up a howl. This caused Mrs. Wiggins to soften her tone slightly.

"I'm prepared to keep the girl till her uncle comes. But don't you try talking me into taking that—that—reprobate under my roof one more night!"

Grabbing the howling Dora, Mrs. Wiggins stormed back towards her buggy. Davy instantly added his protest to Dora's. "Don't take Dora away! Mama said we gotta look after each other," he roared. "You got no right to separate us!"

"Oh, please let Davy stay with me!" pleaded Dora, attempting hopelessly to keep her little feet fixed in one place, while Mrs. Wiggins dragged her away.

The noise brought Rachel and Mr. Drabble onto the veranda. Seeing Mrs. Wiggins mounting the buggy with only one child in tow, Rachel was seized with a terrible fear that the boy might be left at Green Gables. Quickly she grabbed hold of Davy and shooed him in front of her as she ran after Mrs. Wiggins.

"Oh Mrs. Wiggins, wait!" she called. "You've forgotten the little brat. You can't leave him here! Yoohoo, Mrs. Wiggins!"

"Mrs. Lynde, Mrs. Lynde," cried Mr. Drabble hoarsely. "Pray tell, what am I to do about your casket? We have not yet come to any financial arrangement!"

It seemed to Marilla that if the clamor did not instantly stop she would go mad. Setting her shoulders squarely, she turned on Mr. Drabble. "Mr. Drabble," she said, and there was something in her tone that made him stand up straight and take notice, "no one in this house is going to buy a casket, now or in the near future. Kindly leave this house at once."

Abandoning Davy, Rachel rushed back to protect her distinguished guest. But it was too late. Whatever gumption Mr. Drabble had managed to muster for his morning's enterprise faded under Marilla's look of fury. Meekly he gathered up his gladstone bag, doffed his hat to the assembled company and crept away.

"Marilla Cuthbert," fumed Rachel, "that's my solid oak coffin with the mauve whatcha-ma-call-it riding off with that man. All I'm trying to do is die with a little style. Why must you spite me to my face?"

Davy, who had been studying Rachel with the detached curiosity of a budding scientist, now piped up. "Say, what's wrong with yer face, Ma'am? It's all puffed up like a pumpkin."

Rachel's color deepened. "You're not thinking of taking in these hooligans, are you, Marilla?" she hissed. "Because I'm warning you. Orphans are dangerous. You haven't forgotten that child from the orphanage who put strychnine in the well, have you? He came to a sticky end, remember? And so did those unfortunate people who took him in. The agonies they suff—"

"Just a minute, Rachel," interrupted Marilla. Mrs. Wiggins was turning the buggy. Any minute now she would be riding away with Dora. But there was no stopping Rachel once she was launched.

"Now I know Anne Shirley turned out to be harmless. But that was a long time ago, Marilla. And you had a narrow escape. Between you and me and the bedpost, you won't be so lucky twice—Marilla!!"

For the second time that day, Marilla had simply turned her back and run away as Rachel was speaking. Regardless of her years and girth, she was pounding after Mrs. Wiggins's buggy as though her life depended on catching up to it.

"Stop, Mrs. Wiggins!" she cried, waving her arms. "Mrs. Wiggins, come back!" Mrs. Wiggins pulled the cart to a stop and stared down at Marilla's flushed face.

"I cannot turn my back on Mary's children," panted Marilla. "Thank you for all your kindness, Mrs. Wiggins. But I will take both children."

"Are you rightly sure, Miss Cuthbert?"

"Yes...I mean...no! I mean—" amended Marilla, heart yielding to head, "I shall take the children until their Uncle Willy comes to collect them."

"Well, all I can say is, some people is gluttons fer punishment." With this remark, Mrs. Wiggins gathered up the sobbing Dora and deposited her in Marilla's arms. "Good luck to you," she called as she urged the horse on down the drive. "And remember what I said. If that lad don't behave, feed him to the pigs!"

"I'll remember," shouted Marilla. "And thank you again, Mrs. Wiggins."

Clasping the little girl in her arms, she turned back to face Rachel.

Chapter Ten

"Laws, Marilla," Rachel moaned, as Mrs. Wiggins's buggy disappeared down the drive. "Must you deliberately set out to rile me! You can't just invite two little guttersnipes into our home! Lord knows what evil they're capable of! Why, one look at them was enough to strike fear into Mr. Crabble's heart. Such a distinguished man, too. Didn't he remind you just the teeniest bit of dear Ambrose? You can't expect a gentleman like that to cope with *children*. No wonder he took off the way he did. And my casket along with him!"

Marilla did not reply. Setting Dora down gently, she dispatched the two children to the pump to wash their tear-stained faces. The truth was, she was not completely sure how to answer Rachel's accusations. Perhaps she *was* being foolish. Indeed, she felt overcome at the rashness of her behavior. Would she be able to cope with two small children even for a short while? Yet what was she to do? Was she to watch as the children were separated? Was she to allow Dora to be driven, sobbing, away from her only brother, having just the other day buried her mother? No, foolish she might well be, but better foolish than heartless.

"Just look at me," lamented Rachel. "Expecting at any moment to meet my Maker! And what do you do? You let those little monkeys snatch my coffin out from under me. Well, all I can say is, I had dark forebodings when you took in Anne Shirley, and now I expect them to be horribly fulfilled."

"Taking Anne in was the finest thing I ever did in my life," flashed Marilla. "I never, ever, for one moment regretted it. And if you can't think of a single cheerful thing to say, then for heaven's sake stop speaking."

Rachel clamped her lips together, turned on her heels and marched into the house. She sulked in her room, quiet as the grave, while Marilla prepared the evening meal.

When the table was set, Mrs. Lynde consented to sit with Marilla and the children, but she refused to speak, although it was evident that she found some of Davy's antics hard to swallow.

"Say, that's a real nice pig," he said, squirming round on his seat to get a better look out the window at the Harrisons' pig. "Can I let him in, Aunt Marilla? I want to pat him."

"Certainly not," retorted Marilla, helping Dora to

peas. "And please call me Miss Cuthbert, Davy. I am not your aunt."

"Ain't decided what to call my frog neither." Davy placed his favorite pet on the table beside his plate. "But he's real hungry, too."

A small yelp escaped Rachel's sealed lips. If there was one thing she loathed above a pig, it was a frog.

"Pigs and frogs don't eat at the same table as people, boy!" she snapped. "Your uncle Willy won't take too kindly to frogs with his dinner."

"Oh, he don't care," replied Davy imperturbably. "He lets his dog eat off his plate, and his cat, too."

"Davy, put that frog away this minute," ordered Marilla. "And don't gobble your food. Can't you be more polite?"

"I'm that famished, I ain't got time to eat mannerly," replied Davy. "'Sides, I ain't had chicken in so long, I clean forgot how good it tastes." He was eating with such relish that Marilla lacked the heart to take him to task, either for his table manners or for his grammar.

She turned her attention to Dora, who sat quietly beside her. "Dora, would you like another helping of chicken, too?"

"No thank you, Miss Cuthbert," replied Dora politely.

"*I'll* have some, thank you, Marilla." Her vow of silence once broken, Rachel saw no reason to resume it. "Even though you didn't think to offer *me* any more."

Marilla refrained from reminding Rachel that only that morning she had claimed to be unable to eat at all. "Please pass the potatoes to Mrs. Lynde, Davy," she said, with remarkable restraint.

"Why should I? She's already got three helpings and I've only got one."

"Just do as I say."

Davy reluctantly held out the bowl while Rachel helped herself to several heaping tablespoons. As she tucked into the potatoes, Davy again studied her intently. Finally he asked, "Why is it you never smile, Mrs. Lynde?"

Rachel glared at him. "I smile," she snapped, her mouth full, "when there is something to smile about. I see nothing funny at this table."

For the rest of the meal, Davy maintained a thoughtful silence. Dora, having polished her plate and licked her knife and fork clean, sat back with a contented sigh. "Thank you for supper, Miss Cuthbert," she said. "We ain't used to chicken *and* potatoes. And we ain't had dessert in ages, not since Mama took sick. Mrs. Wiggins never made dessert. Folks say Mrs. Wiggins is so tight-fisted she wouldn't give a rope to a drowning man. What does that mean, Miss Cuthbert?"

"I think you should be grateful to Mrs. Wiggins no matter what she fed you. She behaved right neighborly, taking you in and looking after you when your poor mother died." Marilla glanced over at Davy, who had disappeared under the tablecloth. "Davy Keith, either sit up straight or leave the table immediately."

Davy emerged from under the cloth, his face flushed. "I dropped my frog," he murmured, casting a sideways look at Mrs. Lynde.

Rachel failed to notice. She stared stonily ahead, trying to conquer a mounting feeling of resentment. How could Marilla pay so much attention to these little horrors when her oldest friend was pining away with a toothache? "I suppose I'll just have to get my own ginger tea, since you're so busy, Marilla," she said huffily, rising from the table, martyrdom written in every gesture. Head high, she took one step forward and fell flat on her face. There she lay, emitting strange little squawks, unable to rise.

Davy and Dora burst into howls of laughter. Marilla rushed to help her friend. As she lifted her to her feet, she noticed that the laces of one of Rachel's shoes had been tied to the leg of the table.

"Davy Keith!" exploded Marilla, "You apologize to Mrs. Lynde at once. How could you do such a terrible thing?"

"I only wanted to make her laugh," sputtered Davy. "She said nothing was funny, see? Wasn't it funny when she fell on her fanny?"

"You go right now and scour your tongue with soap and water! Besides, Mrs. Lynde fell on her face. And it wasn't the least bit funny. Now off to bed, the pair of you."

Little snorts of laughter escaped from the brother and sister as they climbed down off their chairs and headed upstairs.

Rachel glowered after them. It looked like a fight to the finish between these monstrous twins and herself. But when it came to battles, Rachel was a hardened veteran. She would have no trouble in sending them both packing from Green Gables. Then she could relax and plan her funeral in peace and quiet.

Chapter Eleven

While getting ready for bed, Rachel mustered the arguments she would present to Marilla as to why the children should be sent away the following day. "Now no moaning and groaning this time," she warned herself in the dressing-table mirror. "Nor no foot-stamping neither. Cold logic, that's what you need, my girl. Cold logic and some of that let-me-get-straight-to-the-point-Your-Honor tone. Just like in them newspapers."

Rachel always read the Boston newspapers for the murder trials. Elbows on the kitchen table, hands propping up her head, she would read bits aloud to the empty kitchen. She loved the round, satisfying sound of the legalistic phrases. "I draw the Court's attention," she would repeat to the stove. Turning to the kettle she would hiss "while in full possession of his faculties," pulling what she thought of as an appropriately solemn face and inspecting it in the kettle's copper surface.

Now, as she slapped buttermilk all over her cheeks and forehead to keep her skin looking young, she muttered suitable words over and over. "Sacrifice...duty..." she whispered. "Duty to the children and yourself." There lay a good line of argument. Marilla's devotion to duty was legendary. If only Rachel could make her see that her duty lay in having the children adopted by someone younger, she would have won the battle. A younger couple would be ideal, a childless couple who had always wanted children. Why, they would look on Marilla as a benevolent angel. They would devote their energy to raising those children. "They'd turn them into solid, upright citizens," Rachel said aloud, her sense of the rightness of it all growing by the minute. "They'd be the making of those poor orphans. Why, Marilla, it'd be right selfish of you to stand in their way."

Excited as she was, it was hard for Rachel to avoid splashing buttermilk on the bandage around her chin. In the darting candlelight, she peered at her

❧❧❧

It looked like a fight to the finish between
those monstrous twins and Rachel.

❦❦❦

Rachel snatched her hand away from Marilla.
Her color deepened from red to purple.
"How dare you!" she screamed. "Well, I'm not going!
Wild horses wouldn't drag me there...."

❧

The newly corseted porker careened across the yard...

❧❧❧

"Anyone with half a mind can see
these children belong here."

reflection with unseeing eyes, her attention absorbed by the debate taking place in her mind. She failed to notice how odd she looked, standing there in her bare feet, her jaw swollen, her forehead and cheeks caked in buttermilk. Using both hands, she patted the yellowish liquid under her raised chin with an upward, hand-over-hand motion, her mouth contorted in a grimace of concentration.

Five minutes later, having slipped into her flannel nightgown, she waylaid Marilla on the upstairs landing.

"Mercy me! How you startled me!" exclaimed Marilla as the bulky figure, smelling strongly of sour milk, darted out of the shadows.

Marilla had been about to enter Anne's old room, which had been assigned to Davy. Seeing Rachel, and guessing her intent, she pushed the half-opened door shut in a quick, protective motion. This simple action infuriated Rachel. It made her feel as though Marilla were excluding her from the new way of life which was already beginning to form around the children. Forgetting all about her resolve to adhere to well-reasoned argument, she nodded furiously in the direction of Davy's room.

"That boy!" she hissed. "That boy needs a birch switch took to his backside."

"Rachel! Calm yourself."

But Rachel, feverish and exhausted, had loosened

the floodgates, and there was no stopping the flow of words. "I declare, you have me wore to a fiddle-string, Marilla," she panted. "Can't you see I'm failing fast? I know I won't get a wink of sleep for worrying about what that young criminal might get up to next. Why, we might all be murdered in our beds!"

"That 'criminal' as you call him is seven years old, Rachel. Besides, you heard what I told Mrs. Wiggins. They're only staying here till their Uncle Willy comes."

"Are you trying to tell me you'd send them to Uncle Willy? Uncle Willy, who lets the dog eat off his plate?" Rachel had by now strayed so far from her original purpose that she could barely remember what it was. "From what I've heard about Uncle Willy, I'd say Davy Keith is the spitting image of him. It wouldn't surprise me one bit to catch that boy barking at the moon."

Marilla studied the smeared cheeks and inflamed jaw. "Go to bed now, Rachel," she said quietly. "Your tooth is making you feverish. If you don't do something about it tomorrow, I shall have to take matters into my own hands."

"Don't you try to sidetrack me, Marilla. I want those children out of this house, do you hear me? You're too old to be waiting on them hand and foot. You should be setting your mind on higher things."

"Like caskets, I suppose?"

"Yes, like caskets. There's a lot to be said for

death, when you think about it. Imagine all the trouble we'd have been spared if you and me had died young. I wouldn't have this pesky toothache. Mr. Crumble would never have taken to his heels with a flea in his ear. And those children wouldn't be pestering us now."

"Go to bed, Rachel," repeated Marilla, taking her friend's elbow and steering her gently towards her room. "You have a good sleep and everything will be much better in the morning."

"If I'm alive in the morning," muttered Rachel darkly, but she allowed herself to be guided through her door and into bed.

It was past eleven by the time Marilla managed to get herself to bed. She had put Dora to sleep in her room, thinking that the twins might sleep better if they were separated for the night. Then she had returned downstairs to see to the dishes and to lay the table for breakfast the next morning.

As she placed her candle on the night table beside her bed, Marilla gazed at the sleeping child. The long eyelashes curled downwards towards her cheeks, casting a tiny shadow on the round, gently breathing face. One chubby hand lay open and upwards, flung backwards onto the pillow against a tangle of yellow curls. Marilla caught her breath. She looked so tiny, so vulnerable, and yet already she had lost both father and mother. At that moment, Dora stirred and opened her eyes. She looked up at Marilla, searching her face, as though trying to read something there. Then she closed her eyes and, with a little sigh, turned over on her side.

Marilla felt instantly cast down, as if she had already failed the child. "What's the matter, Dora?" she whispered. "Can't you sleep?"

Again, the child's head turned. She spoke so softly that Marilla had to bend closer to catch her drift. "My Mama...she used to kiss me every night before I went to sleep."

Relief flooded Marilla. Here was something she *could* do. Had she not kissed her own Anne every night before she went to bed? Stooping, she placed a kiss on the child's forehead. "There now," she said. "Now you can sleep snug as a bug in a rug."

A smile glimmered on the child's face and in a second she had fallen back into a deep sleep.

Almost overcome with weariness, Marilla went to the washstand and washed her face in cold water, then brushed out her hair. Just as she was slipping off her shoes, Davy came hurtling through the door.

"Shhh, child! You'll wake your sister! Why, whatever's the matter?" Tears were spilling down Davy's cheeks.

"I had a bad dream," sobbed the child, flinging himself so hard at Marilla he almost knocked her backwards. "I dreamed a big fat ghost with a giant layer-cake for a head chased me all round my bed. He was so big, I couldn't even stick my fork in him!"

"Davy, Davy! Don't you know there are no such things as ghosts?"

"'S'posin' there is, though, Miss Cuthbert? Couldn't I just stay here with you and Dora? Just in case? Please?"

"There isn't room for all three of us, Davy. Now you be a brave boy and go back to bed. Go on now."

Davy hesitated. "It ain't easy bein' brave at night, Miss Cuthbert," he gulped. "It's a lot easier when the sun's out."

"Run along, Davy. I'll come and tuck you in."

"Miss Cuthbert...see...maybe I could be brave if..."

"If what, Davy Keith?"

The words came out in a rush. "If someone would hug me first."

Marilla reached over and took the little boy in her arms. "There," she said, giving him a warm hug. "Do you feel braver now?"

"Much braver. Only..."

"Only what, Davy?"

"Only why don't Mrs. Lynde like me, Miss Cuthbert? I thought I could make her laugh, see?"

"But instead you hurt her feelings with that silly trick."

"I'm sorry now I did it."

"Being sorry isn't good enough, Davy. You'll have to pray to God for forgiveness."

A fresh batch of tears welled up in Davy's eyes. "I ain't talkin' to God no more," he mumbled.

"Davy Keith, what a wicked thing to say!"

"He don't listen to little children. He don't think we're important enough."

"That's not true, Davy. Wherever did you get such an idea?"

"He took my Mama away, didn't he? And my Papa before that. If he thought me and Dora was important, why'd he go and do a thing like that?"

Marilla's gaze softened. Again she put her arms around Davy. "I know how much you must miss your mother, Davy. But she was in such a lot of pain, it would have been very hard for her to go on living."

The tears fell openly now. "I know. She was awful sick. She told me she was glad to die and that I shouldn't be sad. But I can't help bein' sad, Miss Cuthbert. It just sneaks over me."

"Did your Mama say anything else, Davy?"

"She said I was to look after Dora and always stand up for her, and I will, too. An' she said I was to be a good boy. Only it ain't easy bein' good when you're sad, Miss Cuthbert. And then...and then..."

"And then what?"

"And then that Mrs. Lynde, she just hates me. I know it."

"Nonsense, of course Mrs. Lynde doesn't hate you. But she might like you a lot better if you were kinder to her. She's not herself these days."

"Who is she, then? I want to know!"

"That's just a manner of speaking, Davy. What I mean is, her tooth's bothering her. If she'd only have it pulled!"

The scientist appeared again through the tears in Davy's eyes. "I got a loose tooth," he said, brightening. "I been watchin' it wiggle. You want to see it wiggle?"

"No, I do not want to see it wiggle. I want to see you go back to bed."

"I will, Miss Cuthbert. Only, why won't Mrs. Lynde have her tooth pulled, if it'll make her all better?"

"I'm not sure, Davy. I think she's afraid."

"Afraid of what?"

"Afraid it will hurt more to have it pulled than it does now. And that's why you must think of ways to be nicer to her. Now, that's enough talk for tonight. Back to bed. Here's one more hug to keep bad dreams away."

Davy smiled up at Marilla. "You're a lot nicer than Mrs. Wiggins, Miss Cuthbert, even if you are old. I'll bet you wouldn't whip a boy just 'cause he can't keep still. Can't a boy be just as good runnin' round as keepin' still? I want to know."

"Bed, Davy Keith."

This time Davy trotted obediently to the door,

where he turned, rubbing his eyes. "You won't forget to tuck me in, will you?"

"I won't forget."

"You know what, Miss Cuthbert? I'm gonna try real hard to be good. I'll be so good you won't know it's me."

"Good night, Davy."

Five minutes later, when Marilla tiptoed into his room to tuck him in, Davy was fast asleep.

Chapter Twelve

The next afternoon, Marilla was bent over a steaming tub, scrubbing the children's dirty clothes on the washboard, when she heard Rachel shriek at the top of her lungs. In another second she came striding in to the kitchen from the veranda, clutching the Avonlea *Chronicle*.

"Would you take a look at this!" she screeched, thrusting the newspaper at the astonished Marilla. "That Olivia King should be strung up!"

"You know I can't read a thing without my glasses. What on earth's the matter?"

"Ambrose Dinsdale. That's what's the matter. Olivia King's written a whole piece about him. Right here, for everyone in the world to gawk at." Rachel's finger jabbed at the offending page. "I blame you for this, Marilla. I would have taken my broken heart silently to the grave, but you had to prompt that snippet's curiosity!"

"If I've told you once, I've told you a hundred times, Rachel. I had no idea you'd kept his portrait. That's what piqued her interest."

"Why shouldn't I keep his portrait? I had every right to it, didn't I? I could have been Mrs. Ambrose Dinsdale right now if you hadn't forced me to marry Thomas Lynde. I've always been faithful to his memory, poor soul. But I was never happy."

Rachel pulled an enormous handkerchief out of her sleeve and attached it to her nose. Her usually well-disciplined hair stood out in rebellious wisps against her flushed face.

Marilla gave silent thanks she had taken steps to ensure that Rachel would see Dr. Blair that afternoon. Rachel in one of her moods was bad enough, but Rachel with an infected tooth and a fever was enough to try the patience of a saint. Still, relief was near at hand. Knowing this, Marilla was able to keep her tone level.

"I had nothing to do with your marrying Thomas, Rachel," she said reasonably. "That was completely your decision. I merely gave you a word of advice, that is all. Besides, Thomas worshipped the ground you walked on." More fool he, she felt like adding.

Rachel's eyes were wet. "Nobody loved me like Ambrose Dinsdale. I should never, never have let you influence me, Marilla. When I think of the nights I've cried myself to sleep over Ambrose." Her shoulders heaved with emotion.

"Rachel, for pity's sake, have some sense!"

The sound of shattering glass from the floor above interrupted what might have developed into a bitter argument. Silenced, both women stared up at the ceiling.

As soon as he heard their footsteps on the stairs, Davy braced himself for the pain. He knew it would come, but he did not feel in the least bit scared. More important was finding out about a whole mess of things. He would find out if the mechanism he had rigged up worked. He would find out how the pain felt. Most of all, he would find out if he could make Mrs. Lynde like him. He sat up straight on the edge of the bed. At his feet lay the shattered mirror. He was sorry to have to break it. It was awful pretty. He hoped Miss Cuthbert would understand that some things had to get broke if a fellow was ever to make discoveries.

"I might have known it," he heard Rachel say outside the door. "It came from Anne's old room, where that little wretch is sleeping."

The next moment the door was wrenched open. Davy felt a sharp pain in his gum. Then the blood was seeping into his mouth. It tasted, he noted, like warm, salty butter.

"Davy Keith!" exclaimed Marilla, who was just in time to see a tooth pop out of Davy's mouth and fly across the room, attached by a string to the door handle.

With a yell Davy was on his feet. Grasping the dangling tooth he held it out triumphantly to Rachel. "This here's for you Mrs. Lynde!" he panted, a trickle of blood appearing on his lip. "It's a present. Miss Marilla told me as how you're too skeered to get your tooth pulled. So I figured I'd show you it ain't so bad." He held the small, bloodied object out towards Rachel, who shrank back. "You can keep it, if you want," he added generously.

"I wouldn't touch it with a barge-pole!" shuddered Rachel.

"Take the tooth, for heaven's sake, Rachel. The child's only trying to be kind."

"Kind! I'll give him kind! Just look at that mirror in smithereens on the floor. That's seven years bad luck right there."

"I don't want you stuffing the child's head with superstitious nonsense, Rachel," admonished Marilla, surveying the damage with regret. The mirror had been a favorite of Anne's. "If it's an accident, then there's nothing left for us to do but clean it up."

"It weren't no accident, Miss Marilla," piped up Davy. "I did it on purpose, so's you'd come up here and yank my tooth. And that's just zackly what happened." He beamed. He felt as a real scientist must, whose experiment has just been proved to his satisfaction.

Rachel stared at him aghast. "I'm telling you, Marilla, that child is completely without conscience."

Davy's ears perked up. "What's a conscience? I want to know!"

The question gave Marilla pause. She did not feel entirely qualified to answer. In the absence of a theological expert, she did her best.

"Your conscience is in here, Davy," she replied, pointing in the general direction of her heart, an area where she had always imagined the soul to be.

Davy stared at her. "Where?" he persisted. "I can't see it."

"It's a bit like God, Davy. You can't see Him either. Your conscience is what makes you feel bad when you've done something wrong."

"But what good is it if it don't stop you first? If it just lets you go right ahead an' get in trouble?"

"You have to listen for it, Davy. If you listen hard it will tell you what's wrong before you do it."

"I don't see why you waste your breath on that child, Marilla," snorted Rachel. "Anyone can see he's a lost cause."

Davy was bent over, listening intently to his chest and stomach. Now he raised his head, a worried frown on his face. "I don't hear nothin'," he said. "Maybe I lost mine."

Rachel sighed in exasperation. Her tooth ached even more than usual. She felt in dire need of a strong cup of tea. "Come along, downstairs, Marilla," she said. "I still have a bone to pick with you."

Normally Davy would have wanted to know all about the kind of bone Rachel intended picking, but he was too preoccupied with his missing conscience to pay strict attention. A thought struck him suddenly. "What happens if your conscience slips?" he asked. "Why, it'd fall right smack into your stomach, wouldn't it?" He turned and headed for the door.

"Where do you think you're going now?" demanded Rachel, grabbing him by the arm.

"I'm goin' straight back down to that outhouse, Mrs. Lynde. I'm gonna have a real good look out there. 'Cause maybe that's where I lost my conscience. It could've slipped out when I was doin' my business."

"Davy Keith, if you go near that outhouse I'll give you a good walloping!"

"But if I don't find my conscience, how 'm I ever gonna be good? An if I ain't good, you ain't never gonna like me!"

The hazel eyes looking up at Rachel were filled with anxiety. The arm she had grabbed still held the rejected tooth clutched in its grubby hand. She remembered how he had come running towards her, holding out his prize, his eyes dancing with triumph. He had offered it to her, proudly, as though it were a gift. All the anger drained out of Rachel. She felt mean and strangely sad. She let go of Davy's arm.

"Go outside and play, child," was all she said. "But don't let me catch you spending a minute more than you need to in that outhouse."

Chapter Thirteen

Marilla swept up the shards of broken glass and hurried downstairs to finish the washing. Sara and Olivia would be arriving shortly, and she wanted to have everything done before they came. In her hurry, she barely had time to find her glasses and skim over Olivia's article in the Avonlea *Chronicle*, but from what she read, she could find no cause for Rachel's outburst.

Glancing out the window, she saw Dora sitting on the grass, engaged in deep conversation with the Harrisons' kitten. Davy was nowhere to be seen. Marilla profoundly hoped he was not dismantling the outhouse in search of his conscience. As she wrung out the clothes, she could not help smiling. There was no denying that since Davy Keith's arrival, there had not been a dull moment at Green Gables.

Picking up the laundry basket, Marilla walked outside to the clothesline. A fresh breeze had set the apple trees dancing. A good drying day, she thought to herself, glad to be out of the house and away from Rachel's complaints. She had not spent more than five minutes at the line when she heard familiar footsteps approaching over the grass.

"What am I going to do about that article? That's what I'd like to know. I'm so mad with Olivia King, I could shake her!" Snatching up a towel, Rachel flapped it so viciously that it showered Marilla with drops.

Marilla sighed. Any minute now Olivia and Sara would turn up, and then she would be free to escort Rachel to Dr. Blair's surgery. Of course, she hadn't yet told Rachel about this plan. Why get her riled up sooner than was absolutely neccessary? The mere thought of breaking the news to her friend made Marilla's pulse quicken. Fighting down a feeling of panic, she took the towel and hung it on the line with the others.

"There's no need to take on so, Rachel," Marilla said. "Olivia never mentioned your name. She merely refers to Ambrose Dinsdale and his Touring Evangelical Choir. I don't see what's so dreadful about that. After all, the choir was very popular in its day."

Rachel sniffed. She felt so confused, she barely knew what she felt. It was true that Olivia had not linked her name with that of Ambrose Dinsdale. But somehow this annoyed as well as relieved her. She felt hot and angry. Closing her eyes, she took several deep breaths, trying to calm herself.

Marilla reached into the laundry basket and shook out Rachel's corset. She was pegging it on the line when Davy, his arms and legs covered with mud, wandered up.

On his way to the outhouse in search of his conscience, he had been distracted by the sight of the pond. The thought suddenly occurred to him that he could build a dam. His brain filled with designs and plans worthy of a master beaver and he splashed around happily, searching for suitable rocks. When the supply ran out, he decided to look farther afield. He was making his way towards Marilla's rock garden when he caught sight of a large, damp, pink thing hanging from the line.

"Hey, what's that?" he asked, staring at the corset.

"That," replied Marilla, "is a bandage for fat people." She glanced over at Rachel, a smile in her eyes.

"Why do fat people need bandages?" asked Davy, this latest cause for speculation draining all thoughts of dams from his brain.

"Get away from my corset!" snapped Rachel, glowering at both Davy and Marilla.

"I only wanted to look at it." Davy scrutinized the strange pink object with the dangling laces. "What's it for?"

"Fat people use them to make their fat disappear," ventured Marilla, hoping to tease a smile out of Rachel.

"But where does the fat go after you put the bandage on?" The scientist in Davy was intrigued.

"It's...um...well, it's magic," smiled Marilla. "It just goes *poof* and disappears."

"Poof?" asked Davy doubtfully.

"Poof, Davy. Poof, Poof, POOF!!"

"Marilla Cuthbert! I thought you warned *me* not to fill that child's head with nonsense," huffed Rachel. "At least I care enough about my appearance to *wear* a corset, not like some I could mention. If you ask me—"

But no one ever did ask Rachel, for at that moment Olivia and Sara appeared on the veranda, waving their arms and hallooing. Marilla's face lit up in a smile of relief. Quickly she pinned the last of the children's clothes up to dry and hurried towards Sara and her aunt. But Rachel had reached them first. Already she was shaking her index finger in Olivia's face.

"I demand a retraction!" she cried, her voice hoarse with emotion.

Olivia's smile vanished. "A retraction, Mrs. Lynde? But I didn't even print your name!"

"No, you didn't, and I'm extremely cross with you. I mean...Never mind that! You mentioned Ambrose's name. You've stirred up a hornet's nest. I want you to clear my name, and I want you to do it immediately! Do I make myself clear?"

Olivia and Sara gaped at Mrs. Lynde. Was her

mind wandering? Or had it disappeared completely?

Behind Rachel, Marilla gestured to the two girls to pay no attention. "She's not herself," she mouthed, and she pointed to her own mouth to remind them of Rachel's toothache.

Olivia nodded in understanding. "We didn't come about the article, Mrs. Lynde," she said, turning her attention back to Rachel. "We came about the doctor."

"The doctor? What doctor? What are you talking about? Did you slander a doctor, too?"

Marilla steeled herself for a scene. She reached out and took Rachel's hand gently. "Now I don't want you getting all worked up, Rachel," she said. "But I was so worried about your health I got up early this morning and called on Dr. Blair. He's agreed to see you this afternoon. Then I stopped by Rose Cottage and arranged for Sara to stay with the children while we're out."

Rachel snatched her hand away from Marilla. Her color deepened from red to purple. "*You* arranged!" she screamed. "How dare you! How dare you think you can arrange my life! Well, I'm not going! Wild horses wouldn't drag me there, and that's my final word on the subject!" She flounced into the house, slamming the screen door behind her.

"Stand back, ladies," murmured Marilla. "This is something I shall have to deal with on my own." So saying, she hurried in after Rachel and closed the door.

Sara looked over at Olivia. "This may take a while, Aunt Olivia," she remarked. "May I go play with the twins while we're waiting? I'd like to get to know them better."

"Of course. I think I'd better get the buggy ready, just in case Marilla wins the battle." Aunt and niece descended the front steps, leaving Miss Cuthbert alone with her difficult friend.

After the bright light outside, it seemed dark in the front parlor. Marilla could barely make out Rachel's form in the rocker by the window. She stood still in the doorway, listening to the angry, rhythmic creak of the chair and the short, rapid bursts of her friend's breathing.

"Now listen to me, Rachel," she said quietly. "That tooth is poisoning your whole system. If you don't have it out, it could kill you."

"Good!" sniffed Rachel. "I'd be better off dead. At least I wouldn't be reminded at every turn of Ambrose and what I've missed."

"That's as may be. But you can't die before you've ordered a suitable casket, now can you? You know how you like to keep up appearances."

"And who's fault is that, pray?"

"It's mine, I know. I should never have asked Mr. Drabble to leave before you had settled matters with him. But I'll make it up to you, Rachel. If you come quietly with me now, and if you still feel the same after you've seen Dr. Blair, then I shall write to Mr. Drabble myself and invite him back straight away." Marilla swallowed hard. "Why, I may even order my own casket from him at the same time."

Rachel sat up straight. "You would?"

"If you ask me. Then yes, I will."

Rachel found her handkerchief and blew her nose loudly. Taking this as a positive portent, Marilla hastened to fetch her friend's coat and hat. Then, holding Rachel's arm, she walked her out to the buggy, where Olivia sat waiting. In silence they mounted and drove off.

The children watched them go. "Poor Mrs. Lynde," said Davy. "She sure do look glum. An' it's all my fault."

"Why is it your fault, Davy?" asked Sara, who felt drawn towards the chubby orphan with his persistent questions.

"I tried to show her it don't hurt much having your tooth yanked, but I jes' couldn't make her believe me."

"Maybe she'll believe Dr. Blair. What is it, Dora?" Dora was pulling at Sara's sleeve.

"I wanna show you the kitten," whispered the little girl, slipping her sticky hand into Sara's cool one and pulling her towards the barn.

Davy followed them, kicking at pebbles as he went. "I jes' wish," he muttered, "I jes' wish I could think of somethin' to make that Mrs. Lynde like me."

Chapter Fourteen

The late-afternoon sun shot arrows of scarlet through the high barn window. In streams of rainbow dust, they arched onto the hay, which glowed as though lit by stained glass. Sara breathed in the warm, drowsy atmosphere. "Barns always remind me of the nicest kind of churches," she sighed. "They're so peaceful. I think this barn is pure heaven."

"Mrs. Wiggins says our Mama's in heaven," announced Dora, who had found the kitten and was dragging it towards Sara by its hind paws.

"Where is heaven, Sara?" asked Davy, puckering up his nose. "I want to know."

Sara thought for a moment. "I'm not sure exactly. I've always imagined it to be up there." She pointed upwards towards the sky, which, seen through the small barn window, seemed radiant with crimson and gold.

"Do you think Mama's up there?" asked Dora, holding the kitten up by its paws to show it the glowing window.

"All good people go to heaven, Dora," answered Sara, rescuing the complaining kitten. "Your mother must be there too."

"What I can't figure is, how'd she climb up?" Davy scratched his thatch of curly hair and wriggled himself deeper into the hay. "I seen them droppin' her into a big hole in the ground. She weren't ever one for climbin', not my Mama. Why, just gettin' up those stairs to kiss us good night made her pant real hard. So how'd she ever climb all that way up there to heaven? I want to know."

Sara leaned back against the fragrant hay, stroking the kitten gently behind the ears. "Perhaps she climbed a golden staircase," she said dreamily, "and flew the rest of the way on angel wings."

"I wonder how I can get angel wings, 'cause I'd sure like to fly up to heaven and tell my Mama to come home."

Sara looked over at Davy. The hurt in his voice brought her own painful memories back. Although she had been much younger than Davy when her mother died, she could still remember that feeling of confusion, of feeling as though a huge hole had been carved in her heart, leaving only emptiness and fear behind.

"I used to want the same thing when my mother died, Davy," she said softly. "At first I was sure I could find her again, somewhere, if only I looked hard enough. I would search and search and fall asleep crying, because I hadn't found her and I thought it was my fault."

A sense of relief washed over Davy, a feeling that he was not alone in trying to solve the huge mystery his life had stumbled into. At the same time, the unaccustomed sympathy in Sara's voice made tears start to his eyes.

"I want her to come home, see?" he said, struggling to keep his voice from breaking down. "I want things to be how they was before she took sick."

"They can't though, Davy. They've changed now."

The tears rolled unchecked down his chubby cheeks. "But I don't *want* them to change. I want them to stay the same. I want her back."

"Davy, think of it this way. Your Mama died. But that doesn't mean she's left you completely."

He stared at her, drops glistening on his eyelashes. "It don't?"

"She's still in your heart. You can still speak to her there. Even though you can't see her. That's how I speak to my mother."

Davy rubbed his wet cheeks with his sleeve. He looked thoughtful. "You mean sorta like my conscience?"

"Better than that," smiled Sara, rising to her feet, still clutching the kitten. She shook the straw from her skirt.

"Say, Sara, you know where my conscience might be? I been looking everywhere for it. You think I mighta dropped it?"

The kitten chose that moment to make its escape. Bounding from Sara's arms it shot away through the hay, followed by a pleading Dora. Not as nimble as the kitten, the little girl stumbled and fell against an old ladder that led to the barn's upper reaches. Sara righted her and the ladder before turning to Davy, who still sat cross-legged in the straw.

"You can't drop your conscience, Davy. It's not as easy as that."

"If I could find the pesky thing, I could be good, see, and then Mrs. Lynde would like me and Miss Marilla wouldn't send us away."

"Is Marilla going to send you away?" The thought made Sara sad.

"She's gonna send us to Uncle Willy. Say, Sara, did you ever meet Uncle Willy's dog? You think dogs got consciences too? Where would they keep 'em, that's what I want to know."

"I think thinking on an empty stomach is bad for the soul," replied Sara, throwing open the barn door so that the warm, early-evening light flooded in. "I think we should cut ourselves slices of Marilla's blueberry pie and eat them on the veranda, while we watch the sun settle itself for sleep. That's what I think. I'll race you both!"

She set off suddenly across the yard, followed by a squealing Dora.

Davy got to his feet, still puzzling over the whereabouts of his conscience. As he emerged from the barn he caught sight of the Harrison's pig trotting happily towards the water trough. An idea flashed into his brain, making him stand stock still, amazed by the sheer simplicity of it.

"Say, Dora! Wait up a second!" he called.

His sister halted, one foot on the veranda step. Sara had already disappeared into the house.

"What's the matter? Where are you going now, Davy?" Sitting down on the step, Dora eyed her brother. He was tiptoeing towards the clothesline, which might have been wild game, and he a hunter hoping to trap it, so stealthily did he creep.

"I jes' figured somethin' out, Dora." Davy's voice was low, as though anxious not to disturb the clothesline. "I wanna get Mrs. Lynde on my side. An' Mrs. Lynde, she hates pigs, see?"

Dora did not see. She waited stolidly for a light to dawn. As she waited, she observed the Harrison's pig ambling away from the trough, its mouth gleaming wetly. In the meantime, Davy had snatched up a spare loop of clothesline and was standing directly underneath the huge mass of whalebone and pink elastic that was Mrs. Lynde's corset. The look in his eye unsettled Dora.

"What're you gonna do, Davy?" she asked uneasily.

"I'm gonna make that fat ol' pig disappear! Just wait, you'll see. I'll make it go POOF!" Leaping up, Davy grabbed the corset. It felt stiffer and heavier than he expected, but it came off the line easily enough. With a whoop and a holler, he set off after the pig, the corset in one hand, the rope in the other.

Glancing over its shoulder, the Harrison's pig blinked its tiny eyes. A human was bearing down on it, waving something pink and yelling. Just as the pink object came flapping down across its back, the pig stepped daintily to one side, sending object and human sprawling in a heap in the wet dirt.

"Hey, pig, wait up!" screamed Davy, lifting his head out of a puddle. "Don't you wanna go POOF?"

Evidently the pig had no intention of obliging. Instead it headed straight for the barn, where it had always found safety before.

Struggling to his feet, Davy raced after it, hope high in his heart. He spotted his prey from the doorway. It had made for the shadowy recesses of the barn, where it had burrowed its snout into a huge bale of hay until only its squiggly tail was visible.

"I've caught you now, pig!" whispered Davy exultantly. Looping one end of the rope around itself, he tied it roughly in a knot, then crept forward until he stood directly behind his victim. A tremor of anxiety shook the pig when it sensed Davy's presence. Raising its head it attempted to pull out of its hiding place and reverse direction, sending clouds of hay flying upwards. Quick as lightning, Davy threw the loop over its head and his leg over its back. He stood there, panting hard, feeling the beast's sides heaving, trying to hold it still by the sheer pressure of his legs. The corset was so unwieldy he had difficulty maneuvering it over the pig's broad back. His fingers fumbled with the laces. All the time he was whispering to the startled animal, trying to calm it down. "Don't move, Mr. Pig. Any minute now, you're gonna disappear. POOF you'll go! Up in smoke! Just like magic, Mr. Pig!"

But the pig had other ideas. With an exasperated snort, it swiveled violently around on its hind legs, knocking Davy off his feet a second time. He tried as hard as he could to hold onto the rope, but the furious animal, outraged by the encumbrance around its middle, took to its heels with such force that the rope flew from Davy's fingers.

From the floor of the barn, he watched the newly corseted porker careen across the yard, knocking Dora into the trough in its haste.

"Go POOF, please Mr. Pig!" wailed Davy. "Just for me, PLEASE!!??"

But Mr. Pig, galloping down the lane towards the village of Avonlea, paid him no heed.

From the yard, Davy could hear splashing, dripping noises as Dora pulled herself out of the trough. His heart sank. Opening his mouth, he screamed after the pig at the top of his lungs.

"If you won't go POOF, you might at least bring that there corset back, ya smelly ol' hog! Whatcha think Mrs. Lynde's gonna do to me when she finds out!!"

Chapter Fifteen

Mrs. Lynde came to an abrupt halt in the middle of Avonlea's main street. On either side, Marilla and Olivia urged her on gently, but Rachel refused to budge. She had caught sight of Dr. Blair's shingle. It was an inoffensive little sign, merely listing the physician's surgery hours and indicating that he was available outside these hours to anyone in distress, but it conjured up in Rachel's fevered brain images of the fate which awaited her inside. She feared that, once seated in Dr. Blair's chair, she would be subjected to unspeakable torture, at the end of which, she would be forced to relinquish a tooth. It had long been a matter of pride to Rachel that all the McNabs had gone to their grave with a full set of teeth. The idea that she might be the first to break that fine tradition seemed almost as painful as the extraction itself.

"I am not going in there. And that's flat, so there's no use trying to railroad me!" she announced.

Olivia and Marilla exchanged worried glances. Olivia inclined her head towards the sidewalk, where a cluster of people had gathered, intrigued by the sight of Mrs. Lynde being herded towards the surgery, obviously against her will.

"Mrs. Lynde," whispered Olivia, "people are watching."

"I don't care if the Queen herself is watching. I am not going in."

Plump Mrs. Spencer bustled up, curiosity, disguised as concern, writ large on her features. "Is there anything at all I can help you with, Mrs. Lynde?" she inquired hopefully. Sarah Spencer was known to have a nose for gossip, and at that moment her nose was sending her signals so strong it was positively throbbing.

"You can help me by minding your own business, Sarah Spencer," snapped Rachel.

"Mrs. Lynde has an appointment with Dr. Blair," explained Marilla, anxious to avoid a public squabble. "She needs to have a tooth out."

"Is that all?" Mrs. Spencer's face fell. She had counted on a fatal disease at the very least. "Why, that's nothing. I had two pulled only the other day and I never so much as winced, even though the pain was excruciating. But then, I'm good about pain. I don't believe in making a fuss. Man was born to trouble, remember Rachel, as the sparks fly upwards. Just repeat that over and over while the doctor's doing his worst."

"Thank you, Sarah," murmured Marilla, hastily edging Rachel out of earshot.

The crowd of onlookers had grown. As word leaked out that Mrs. Lynde was on her way to Dr. Blair's for an extraction, people began shouting encouragement and advice.

"Close your eyes. That way you won't see the blood!" shrieked Mrs. Inglis.

"Dr. Blair knows what he's doing. Why, he did an extraction on the McClorys' donkey only last week." This from Mr. Lawson, who had come out from his store to see what all the fuss was about.

Rachel looked pleadingly at Marilla and Olivia. "Make them go away," she begged. "I can't bear to have everyone looking at me."

"The fastest way to get out of the public eye is to walk straight into Dr. Blair's office, Mrs. Lynde," urged Olivia. "Now come along."

The two women took Rachel firmly by each elbow and herded her towards the surgery. As they reached the door, the strangest sound accosted their ears. Children's voices yelled, hooves pounded, and a rising murmur of excitement issued from the crowd on the sidewalk. The three women turned and stared.

"Great heavens!" exclaimed Marilla. "Can that be the Harrison's pig?"

"What on earth is it wearing around its middle?" gasped Olivia. "It looks like...no, it can't be!"

"It's a *corset*!" yodeled Mrs. Spencer gleefully, her eyes raking the faces of the three horrified women who stood as though turned to stone in the street. "But *whose* corset? That's the question!"

Just then Davy, followed closely by Sara and Dora, raced up the street.

"Davy Keith! What is the meaning of this?" Marilla had turned white as a sheet.

Davy lifted a mud-spattered face. "I tried to make the pig disappear, so Mrs. Lynde would like me," he panted. "Only you told a whopper, Miss Marilla! You said Mrs. Lynde's corset was magic, 'cause it makes fat go POOF! But it didn't make the pig go POOF! An' now...an' now..." His voice rose to a wail. "Now you're gonna make ME go POOF 'fore I've even had a chance to find my conscience!"

Mrs. Spencer had edged closer so as better to overhear the conversation. Now she turned back towards her friends on the sidewalk. "I gather," she announced in a stage whisper. "I gather the corset is *Mrs. Lynde's* property. Am I right, Rachel?"

All eyes swiveled in Rachel's direction. But Rachel never gave Mrs. Spencer the satisfaction of a reply, for she had slumped forward in a dead faint. Only the fact that Marilla and Olivia were holding her arms stopped her from collapsing in the dust at their feet.

The next few days passed in a haze of humiliation and pain for Rachel. She felt she would never truly recover from the shock of seeing the Harrisons' pig model her corset down Main Street. Nor did she know how to cure her infected tooth. Having lost consciousness in front of Dr. Blair's surgery, she did not feel inclined to return. Yet she knew she must do something. She could not continue to live with the pain, which now raged inside her jaw like a legion of warring wasps. Neither could she continue to live in the same house as Davy Keith, who had exposed her to public ridicule and caused her to faint.

The arrival, out of the blue, of Uncle Willy's telegram ended her indecision, at least about Davy. Mr. Rooke, the stationmaster, delivered it.

"I got here as fast as I could, Miss Cuthbert," he drawled, holding out the opened envelope, which was addressed to Mrs. Wiggins. "Mrs. Wiggins asked me to bring it on to you. It's from out British Columbia way, from old Ken Keith's brother, Willy. Uncle Willy, he calls himself here. He says—"

"I can read it myself, thank you, Angus." Marilla snatched the telegram from Mr. Rooke and frowned down at it. "I wish they'd make the print a little larger," she said finally. "The letters get all jumbled up. Read it to me, will you, Rachel?"

"'Dear Mrs. Wiggins,'" Rachel read aloud. "'There's no way I can look after a gaggle of children right now. Stop. I'll be back soon as I can. Stop. Willy. Stop.'"

Raising her eyes, Rachel stared at Marilla over the telegram.

In the silence, Mr. Rooke shuffled his feet uneasily. He had hoped for a cup of tea at very least; at very best, several slices of Marilla's famed blueberry pie. He had not counted on being ignored altogether.

"Ahem, uh, well..." He cleared his throat. "I guess I'm a little parched, but I'll get by."

A plague of deafness seemed to have befallen the women. Marilla had snatched the telegram back from Rachel and was again studying it with a blind, baffled look.

"Well, don't bother about me. Parched or not, I can see myself out." Since this declaration was not followed, as he had hoped, by a chorus of protests, Angus Rooke was obliged to let himself out the front door, shutting it with a vengeful bang behind him. Maybe he should stop by the King farm. Granted, he had no telegram to deliver there, but Mrs. King was a generous woman. She could tell just by looking at a fellow whether his stomach was stuck to his ribs for want of a cup of tea or not. Cheered, he hoisted his letter sack onto his shoulder and trudged off down the drive.

Inside Green Gables, Rachel had finally found her tongue. "I knew it all along, Marilla," she declared. "That Willy person had no intention of coming. Why, he's probably locked up in jail, at this very minute. You're stuck with the little brats, that's what. You'd better make up your mind right now to put them out for adoption."

Marilla paled. "I can't do that," she whispered.

"And please lower your voice, Rachel. I won't have you speaking of the children in that manner." Davy and Dora, alerted by the stationmaster's knock, had crept into the front hall and were listening to every word that passed between the two women. The knowledge that their fate was being decided caused even Davy to preserve an awed silence.

It was then that Rachel saw what she must do. "Either that boy goes, or I go, Marilla," she said. Her voice had the ring of finality. "You must choose now, between me or him. I refuse to spend another night under the same roof as that little hooligan."

"You can't ask me to choose between blood relations and you!" exclaimed Marilla. In her distress, she put a protective arm about the twins.

Her gesture made Rachel's blood boil. "I see you have chosen already," she said. "I must say, it's a bitter pill to swallow, Marilla, seeing how quickly you turn your back on a friendship of over fifty years. But if that's how you feel, then I will move this very day to Mrs. Biggins's boarding house."

Marilla felt as though she had been stabbed though the heart. "Rachel, please. Don't say that!" she begged. But Rachel sailed off to her room to pack.

Marilla sank down on the stairs. To think that only the other week it had crossed her mind to ask Rachel to leave, and now that she was really going, it seemed like the end of the world. Sorrow rose in a wave inside her. For all her faults, she would miss Rachel.

A small hand slipped itself inside Marilla's own. Her eyes misted with tears as she felt, rather than saw, Dora snuggle in beside her on the stair.

"Don't worry, Miss Marilla," she whispered. "We won't leave you alone."

Marilla quickly wiped her eyes with the corner of her apron. She must not break down in front of the children.

Davy had not stayed around to witness Marilla's moment of weakness. A remark Rachel had made prompted him to follow her into her bedroom.

"Say, Mrs. Lynde," he inquired, "How come you think my Uncle Willy's in jail? I want to know."

"You want to know! You want to know!" burst out Rachel, flinging her case on the bed and hurling her clothes at it. "If your tongue wasn't hinged in the middle, my life wouldn't be in ruins now!"

Davy stuck out his tongue and examined it closely, his eyes crossing painfully. "I don't see no hinges," he puzzled. Jumping up on the bed, he touched Rachel on the chin. "Would you stick out your tongue too, Mrs. Lynde?" he asked politely. "I wanna see if your hinges are bigger'n mine."

Although he had been by no means rough, the impact of Davy's fingers on Rachel's inflamed jaw made her reel with pain.

"How dare you!" she screamed. "How dare you jump on my bed and slap my face! You get out of here this minute, you rapscallion! And don't let me catch sight of you ever again, because if I do, I swear I'll tar and feather you!"

The child stared at her for a moment, his face registering genuine fear. Then he jumped off the bed and raced out of the room as though all the demons in hell had been loosed against him.

Chapter Sixteen

Anger propelled Rachel Lynde out of Green Gables, down the lane and into the village of Avonlea. Her case banged against her legs as she galloped along, muttering crossly to herself. Anger had prevented her from bidding Marilla goodbye. After all those years of shelter, she had marched out of Green Gables as if it meant nothing more to her than a waiting room.

It was anger, too, that almost caused Rachel to ignore Olivia King, who was obliged to run after her down Main Street, calling her name aloud.

Mrs. Spencer had been happily engaged in a discussion with Mrs. Inglis concerning who was the worst mother in Avonlea. Now, hearing Rachel's name called, she raised her head, torn between reluctance to abandon a topic so rich in human error, and eagerness to watch Rachel Lynde once again make a fool of herself.

"Look!" she whispered to Mrs. Inglis. "If that isn't Rachel Lynde marching down Main Street, cool as you please. It's a wonder she dares show her face in town after all that's happened. I mean, first she dresses that pig up in her underwear. And then she has her name deliberately linked in the newspaper with that of a minister!"

The two women crossed the street to monitor the conversation between Olivia and Rachel. The former had just handed Rachel the latest copy of the Avonlea *Chronicle.*

"Look, Mrs. Lynde," she beamed. "It only came out the other day, but there's been quite a demand for it already!"

"Don't pester me, child. I'm in a hurry."

"I wouldn't have bothered you, Mrs. Lynde, only I thought you'd be eager to see the retraction. That's what you asked me for, isn't it? A retraction?"

Rachel snatched the paper from Olivia and scrutinized the marked column. Her voice rose in horror. "'Olivia King regrets to inform her public that Mrs. Rachel Lynde does not wish to disclose any information whatsoever about the Reverend Ambrose Dinsdale.'"

Mrs. Spencer dug her elbow happily into the midriff of Mrs. Inglis. "One look at her face says it all!" she hissed. "I knew it all along! There's no smoke without a fire. Obviously there's more to this retraction than meets the eye!"

For a brief second, fury deprived Rachel of speech. Then it returned with a vengeance.

"How dare you, Olivia King!" she shouted. "I am going to sue you for *habeas corpus!*"

"*Habeas corpus?* What's that got to do with anything?"

"Plenty, my girl. Don't think you can pull the wool over my eyes. I read them Boston papers. I know all about murder trials. Them lawyers are always suing people for *habeas corpus*, and that's what I fully intend to do with you!"

Turning on her heel, Rachel marched into Mrs. Biggins's boarding house, leaving a dazed Olivia staring after her.

"What's this?" whispered Mrs. Spencer to Mrs. Inglis. "Mrs. Rachel Lynde entering a boarding house? My, my, my, haven't we come down in the world!" With a speed that belied her girth, Mrs. Spencer shot over to peer in Mrs. Biggins's screen door, yanking the hapless Mrs. Inglis after her. Through the wire mesh, Mrs. Spencer could see Rachel rapping on the front desk.

"Come along, Mrs. Biggins!" she was calling. "Hurry up! I need a good room with a clear view of Main Street!"

Mrs. Inglis winced as her midriff once again received the full impact of Mrs. Spencer's elbow.

"Marilla Cuthbert must have thrown that woman out on the street, and good riddance!" breathed Mrs.

Spencer rapturously. "I've always said Rachel Lynde was skim milk pretending to be cream, and I was right."

Mrs. Inglis took the precaution of putting an arm's length between herself and Mrs. Spencer before she replied. "Perhaps Miss Cuthbert has heard about that there retraction," she suggested. "Perhaps she thinks Mrs. Lynde isn't fit to occupy the same house as herself and two innocent children."

"And quite right, too! Why, she's no better than she should be! Who ever would have thought Rachel Lynde would turn out to be the Jezebel of Avonlea!"

Chapter Seventeen

Hetty put her book down in amazement. "Olivia King," she objected. "*Habeas corpus* means that a person who's been arrested has to be brought before a court. It's to prevent people from being imprisoned without being given a legal hearing first."

Olivia sighed impatiently. "*I* know what *habeas corpus* means, Hetty. But I don't think Rachel does. Honestly, I wish we'd never heard of Ambrose Dinsdale. We've had people writing to us from all over the Island inquiring about him. Besides, it doesn't really matter what Rachel takes me to court for. If my editor hears about it, I could lose my job!"

Hetty shifted in her chair. All too clearly she

remembered how Sara and Olivia had come to her after discovering the faded photograph of Ambrose in Rachel's hope chest. She had felt then that the matter should be explored no further. But Olivia had been so keen, so anxious to make a name for herself with her journalism. Besides, Hetty herself had been assailed by a feeling of curiosity about Ambrose Dinsdale. Long suppressed, it had risen inside her, all the stronger for being denied these many years.

"I'll tell you what, girls." Hetty looked down at her long fingers, which she had folded in her lap. "I'll go and talk to Rachel. Perhaps I can persuade her not to pursue this silly idea any further."

"Oh, Aunt Hetty, would you?" breathed Sara. "It would be so terrible if Aunt Olivia were to lose her job."

Olivia's dark eyes shone. "Thank you, Hetty. What a good sister you are to me!"

Hetty said nothing. "I may be a good sister," she thought to herself, "But I'm a foolish old woman all the same."

The very next day, Hetty donned her gray velvet visiting hat and set out on a roundabout route to Mrs. Biggins's boarding house. First, she took the precaution of calling on a distraught Marilla. On hearing what Marilla had to say, she dropped by Dr. Blair's surgery. Following her conversation with him, she returned home and equipped herself with certain items. Only then did she finally return to town to rap on Mrs. Biggins's door and ask to speak with Mrs. Lynde.

A flushed Rachel admitted her. Hetty could see at once that she was feverish. "Rachel Lynde," she admonished the woman with whom she had so often quarreled, "is this how you wish to spend the rest of your life, miserable and alone amongst a great jumble of mismatched furniture and tasteless floor coverings?" She had noticed immediately that the carpet was woven in the most vulgar shades of red and orange.

Rachel attempted to look fiercer than she felt. "If you've come to lecture me, Hetty King," she snapped, "you can leave immediately. I am not one of your pupils, thank heavens!"

She opened the door to show Hetty out, but at that precise moment Dr. Blair appeared. Taking one look at the swollen jaw, he strode into the room before Rachel could stop him.

"That tooth's coming out, Rachel," he said, plopping his black bag down on a chair and removing his coat.

Rachel turned to Hetty. "Did you bring that man with you?" she demanded.

Hetty nodded. "You may thank me later. For the moment, I'll thank *you* to sit down and keep quiet."

Rachel sank onto the side of the bed and stared about her in horror. Everything was happening so quickly, she could barely keep up. Hetty walked to the door and closed it firmly. Then she unpinned her hat, took an apron from her carry-all, shook it out and tied it around her middle. Dr. Blair in the meantime had rolled up his sleeves and was laying out his instruments in a neat pile on one of Rachel's clean towels.

"Not there! Here!" commanded Hetty, pulling Rachel up off the bed and plonking her into a chair that she had positioned in the middle of the room. Rachel opened her mouth to protest, but Hetty immediately shoved a small cloth inside it, so that she had difficulty speaking.

"Arghh!" spluttered Rachel. "Stopr thisr at...arghh!"

Hetty paid no attention. She had whipped out a large napkin and was busily tying it around Rachel's neck.

Dr. Blair stepped up to the patient. "Drink this, Rachel," he ordered. Rachel stared down into a glass of amber-colored liquid. For some reason its smell reminded her of Christmas celebrations and well-scrubbed, boisterous men yarning together on unsteady feet.

"Whatsr?..." she asked suspiciously.

"It's whiskey, Rachel."

"Whiskey!" In one fierce breath Rachel expelled the cloth. "No!" she gasped. "No, I can't. I'm a Temperance woman, Dr. Blair, and you should be ashamed of yourself trying to tempt me!"

There was a knock on the door and Mrs. Biggins appeared bearing a pitcher full of hot water. "There you are, Doctor," she beamed. Her eye fell on Rachel's stricken face. "Now don't you worry none, Mrs. Lynde," she said reassuringly. "It'll all be over before you know what hit you."

Rachel longed to call out to Mrs. Biggins. "Fetch the constabulary," she wanted to scream. "Fetch anyone, the stationmaster, the doctor..." It came home to her then that Dr. Blair *was* the doctor. The door closed behind Mrs. Biggins. Rachel had been abandoned.

She turned beseechingly to Dr. Blair, who was pouring the steaming water into a white china bowl. "Please, Dr. Blair," she whimpered. "I'm an old woman. I can't start knocking back whiskey and waving goodbye to teeth at my time of life."

"Do what you're told, Rachel," said Dr. Blair, washing his hands so vigorously that water splashed onto Mrs. Biggins' combustible carpet. He glanced at Rachel over his shoulder as he dried his hands. "Remember, I am a doctor. That whiskey is medicinal. Now drink it down."

This time Hetty held out the whiskey. Rachel took the glass in her shaking hand. Once again that disturbing smell assailed her. It brought back memories of Christmas puddings, of shouts of laughter, of coming in stamping from the cold after skating parties.

Putting the glass to her lips she gulped the golden liquid down in several long swallows.

"Bravo!" said Dr. Blair. "Now open your mouth."

Outside, on Avonlea's main street, a frisky, mischievous wind had risen. It puffed at the unpaved dirt road, raising startled flurries of red dust. It tweaked the odd leaf loose from the maples and sent it scuttling along the sidewalk. It tugged at the hats of several women who were walking hurriedly along the street, looking left and right as though in search of someone or something. Without exception, they all carried a newspaper. They seemed not to notice the tricks the wind was playing. Almost automatically they clasped their hats onto their heads with one hand while, with the other, they lifted skirt hems out of the flying dust and held onto their newspapers for dear life.

The wind bothered Sara, who hated to get dust in her eyes. Head bent, eyes half shut, she was hurrying over to the newspaper office to meet Olivia when she almost bumped into a woman approaching from the opposite direction.

"Excuse me," the woman panted. "I'm looking for a Mrs. Rachel Lynde. I saw her name in this here newspaper."

Sara opened her mouth to give directions to Green Gables and then suddenly remembered what Olivia had told her. Rachel was no longer living at Green

Gables. She was a resident of Mrs. Biggins's boarding house. At that moment another woman came striding up, holding a copy of the Avonlea *Chronicle*.

"Do you happen to know a Mrs. Lynde, child?"

Sara nodded. Before she could say another word, the first woman had prodded the second with her newspaper. "Mrs. Lynde, did you say? Why, I'm looking for a Mrs. Lynde too!"

"Well, land's sake. Another one! There must be sixteen women behind me, and they're all looking for Mrs. Lynde!"

Sara gasped. Behind the second woman she could see a small army of ladies, marching along Main Street. Each carried what looked like a rolled-up copy of the Avonlea *Chronicle*, as though it were a rifle.

"Yoo-hoo, Sara! Over here!" Sara turned and saw Olivia standing outside Mrs. Biggins's boarding house, surrounded by another phalanx of women. She rushed gratefully over to her aunt.

"What shall I tell these ladies?" whispered Olivia, taking Sara to one side. "They're all looking for Rachel."

"Oh, dear! Do you think it has anything to do with the Reverend Dinsdale, Aunt Olivia?"

Olivia nodded grimly. "I'm afraid so. What a Pandora's box we've opened, Sara!"

"Do you think Rachel will want to see them?"

"She can't see anyone at the moment. She's having her tooth out. Dr. Blair and Hetty are with her now."

As though on cue, a long, high-pitched scream came sailing out the upper front window of Mrs. Biggins's boarding house. It cut through the chatter of the assembled women below, causing them to clutch each other fearfully. They turned their faces upwards towards the window. In silence they waited, as though expecting at any moment to hear another dreadful, heart-stopping cry. But no cry came. Instead, after a pause of several seconds, another sound issued forth. It too was high-pitched, but it did not rise spectacularly and fall lingeringly away, as had the scream. It came in short, staccato bursts. It sounded, thought Olivia, like an inebriated corncrake.

"Why, that's Mrs. Lynde," Sara said suddenly. "That's Mrs. Lynde, and she's laughing!"

Chapter Eighteen

Rachel Lynde opened her eyes and contemplated a new world. It was, she could tell immediately, a world without pain. Gone was that dreadful, throbbing ache, that searing, darting misery that had seemed like nothing less than a wasp's continuous sting. Gone was that knot of anger that had seemed to tie up the outside world into a distorted, hostile place.

She smiled at Hetty, who was holding an ice-pack to her jaw. Strange, Hetty looked different. Not half so fierce. As for Dr. Blair, he was patting her head and holding out a whitish object that reminded her of a tiny onion bulb, roots and all. "Your tooth, Madam," he said with a bow. Rachel grinned and then clapped her hand to her mouth as she felt a tiny breeze dart through the gap in her gums.

"It's gone!" she said, beginning to giggle.

"It's right here," smiled Dr. Blair, popping the tooth into a small jar. "And you can take it home and display it on the mantelpiece, if you so desire."

Rachel's smile faded. *Home.* Why did that word make her heart suddenly drop? Make her feel shivery and bereft all over? Then she remembered. She had left home. Home was no longer Green Gables and Marilla's stern kindness. Home was here. Mrs. Biggins's boarding house. Rachel stared glumly down at the disastrous carpet, her euphoria fading.

Dr. Blair had scrubbed his hands and was shrugging into his jacket. "I'll call in on you in a couple of days, Rachel. You've been lucky, I must say. There's no noticeable damage and the swelling's already going down."

Rachel nodded. "Thank you, Doctor," she said fondly as he turned to leave. Hetty showed him to the door, where he thanked her graciously for all her help.

Rachel huddled on her chair and watched Hetty bustle about the room, setting things to rights. Soon Hetty, too, would be gone and she would be left alone. Again, she shivered. A wickedly cold wind blew in from outside. What *could* she have been thinking of? How could she have walked out on her best friend, just when Marilla needed her most? Standing up to hide her distress, she looked out the window, intending to shut it.

Down below her on the street stood a crowd of women. A snippet of conversation drifted up, in which she caught the name Ambrose Dinsdale. Completely forgetting her present trouble, Rachel moved to one side, where the curtains hid her from view, and listened.

"What do you mean, you're Mrs. Ambrose Dinsdale?" one woman was barking at another. "*I'm* Mrs. Dinsdale."

"I beg your pardon!" interrupted another, outraged. "*My* name is Dinsdale!"

"Piffle!" shrieked another. "You're impostors, all of you! I'm the *real* Mrs. Dinsdale!"

Rachel staggered back. My God, what a fool she had made of herself! But what a worse fool she might be now, had it not been for Marilla!

Clearheaded for the first time in weeks, she thought over the events of so many years ago which had almost caused her to forsake Thomas Lynde, her suitor at the time, and run off with the dashing Ambrose.

"You must examine your conscience, Rachel," Marilla had stated quietly. "Ask yourself who loves and respects you more, Thomas or Ambrose? And whom do *you* respect more?"

Rachel had scoffed at Marilla, muttering that the debonair Ambrose was far more romantic than the steady Thomas. But in her heart she had known Marilla was right. She had sat up late that night in her small bedroom, turning matters over and over in her mind, and by dawn she had rejected Ambrose and chosen Thomas. Instead of eloping with Ambrose, as he had suggested, she had stayed and become engaged to Thomas.

And Rachel had been happy. Thomas had proved a kind, generous husband. Yet somehow Rachel had always held Marilla's advice against her. She blamed Marilla for something she felt she had missed in life. All these years she had thought it was romance. Now she knew it had been danger. Had she married Ambrose, he would have mistreated and abused her—she saw that now. She would have taken her place in an endless line of deceived and abandoned women. Why, at this very minute, she might be down in that street, claiming to be the only wife of a man who clearly had dozens.

"You mustn't stand so long by the window, Rachel. You'll take a chill." Taking Rachel by the arm, Hetty guided her gently back to her chair.

How long had Hetty been standing there, watching? Had she heard what those women were saying? Rachel did not dare express her worries aloud. In silence she allowed Hetty to pull a blanket over her and tuck it in. In silence, she watched the prim, conventional schoolteacher prepare to leave, buttoning up her jacket and pinning on her hat. Her movements brought back a scene Rachel had witnessed long ago, a scene she had forgotten.

It had happened more than fifty years ago, when Hetty and Rachel were slim, young girls. They had always had a prickly kind of friendship, each liking and yet slightly fearing the other.

On this particular evening, Rachel had arrived early for choir practice, hoping to find Ambrose alone. Hearing a noise in the vestry, she had entered quietly. Perhaps she would tiptoe up behind him, put her hands over his eyes, make him laugh.

Ambrose had his back to the door. In any case, he would not have noticed Rachel. He had eyes only for Hetty King, who stood by the vestry mirror, deftly unpinning her new hat. Her hair, which she had not yet started to put up, gleamed chestnut bronze in the soft candlelight. Ambrose was saying something to her, something flattering, Rachel could tell, because Hetty had turned towards him, her eyes dancing with laughter, her cheeks flushed. Then she had seen Rachel. She had raised a hand in greeting, her smile fading. Rachel had stepped into the room and instantly Ambrose had begun to make a fuss over *her*. In the delight of it all, she had forgotten about Hetty. In fact, she had not given

Hetty's feelings towards Ambrose another thought.

Had Hetty entertained hopes of Ambrose, too? Rachel wondered now. She was always so proud, Hetty King, so aware of her family's position. Were she to lose her heart to a charmer like Ambrose, she would hardly admit it to herself, much less to someone like Rachel.

As Hetty turned to leave, Olivia burst into the room. "Mrs. Lynde," she cried. "All those ladies down there are looking for Ambrose Dinsdale! They think you might know where he is. Why, he must have married almost every woman on the Island!"

Rachel pulled herself together. She did not look at Hetty.

"Well, he didn't marry me, that's for sure! Oh, no! Not me! I was on to that Romeo from the very beginning!"

Olivia gazed at Rachel in surprise. "You were? You mean you were never in love with him? What about that photograph? You kept it all these years. Didn't that mean anything?"

Rachel had the decency to blush. "Not a thing," she lied. She turned to Hetty. "We're women of the world, aren't we, Hetty? We know more than to let sweet-talkers like Ambrose bamboozle us, wouldn't you agree?"

Hetty's cheeks, too, were flushed. For a second her eyes searched Rachel's. Great heavens, had Rachel known all along how she felt about Ambrose

Dinsdale? How she, Hetty King, would have followed that man to the ends of the earth, had he but
asked? Only he never asked. And Hetty, mystified by
the strength of her own emotions, had never
breathed a word to anyone, not even to Ambrose
himself. Later, of course, she had seen sense. She had
realized he was nothing but a cheap charmer. But at
the time. Oh, at the time...!

"Don't you agree, Hetty?"

Slowly, Hetty nodded her head. "Of course,
Rachel." Her voice, at first dreamy, quickly gained
strength and briskness. "Reverend Dinsdale may
have been a good-looking man, but it takes more
than good looks to sweep the likes of you and me off
our feet. Olivia, supper will be on the table in half an
hour. Don't be late. As for you, Rachel, if you know
what's good for you, you'll return to Green Gables
with your tail between your legs."

Gathering up her possessions, Hetty swept out of
Mrs. Biggins's boarding house, her head held high.

Chapter Nineteen

Marilla pulled the brush gently through Dora's
glossy curls. She tried not to think about how she
would never brush this child's hair again. Looking on
the positive side, she told herself that she would never

again have to heat kettles of water for the children's baths. Nor need she worry any more about keeping enough food in the house to accommodate Davy's formidable appetite. Never again each night would she climb the stairs, bone-weary, to hear the children say their prayers. As this thought assailed her, she dropped the brush with a little moan. Dora bent to pick it up, handing it back to Marilla with a hug, the type of hug Marilla would soon have to do without.

"Are you feeling poorly, Miss Marilla?" she queried.

"No, child. I'm well, thank you. Just a bit anxious about Miss Carpenter's visit this morning."

"Who's Miss Carpenter?" asked Davy. Arms outstretched, he was wandering around the room shared by Dora and Marilla, trying not to step on the cracks between the floorboards.

"I told you already, Davy. She's the lady from the orphanage. It's very important that both of you make a good impression on her. Otherwise she might decide to send you to separate families. And you want to stay together, don't you?"

Dora's eyes clouded. "We want to stay with *you*," she whispered.

Marilla's heart ached. She knew now, more clearly than she had ever known, that she longed to keep the children. But how could she, an elderly woman with failing sight, manage on her own? Perhaps if Rachel had not moved out, the two of them might have been capable of raising the twins. But Rachel *had* moved out, and Marilla must do as she thought best. She must listen to her head, not her heart. She must do her duty. Surely it was her duty to see the children adopted by younger, more energetic parents?

"Remember, Dora," she quoted. " 'Do your duty, that is best, leave unto the Lord the rest.' I'm trying to do my duty by you."

"I did my duty this morning," muttered Davy glumly, jumping over a large crack and landing by the window, "an' I *still* didn't find my conscience." He pressed his face against the glass, leaving, Marilla noticed, a damp stain where his mouth had rested. "It's all my fault, ain't it, Miss Marilla?" he said. "I make a mess of everything 'cause I'm bad."

"Mrs. Wiggins said if you spit in your shoe at midnight every night, you won't be bad no more," said Dora helpfully.

Davy turned to Marilla. "I know it's mornin' an' all, but couldn't I go to bed straight this minute and start spittin' ?"

"You'll do no such thing, Davy Keith. Besides, you're not bad. You simply haven't learned good sense yet. Now come over here and let me brush that mop of yours. Davy?"

But Davy's attention was wholly taken up by something outside. He stared through the window, his body rigid with fear.

"What is it, Davy?"

"It's Mrs. Lynde! She's come to tar and feather me!"

Rachel stepped briskly along the lane, drawing in great gulps of clean air. The swelling in her jaw had diminished considerably. The pain had not returned. She felt cleansed, renewed. "I may be old," she thought to herself, "but I ain't tired of living yet." If only she could make her peace with Marilla, all would be well. She practiced her speech aloud as she walked. "Marilla Cuthbert," she murmured. "Marilla Cuthbert, I was wrong, and I'm sorry." No, a less direct approach might be better. "Marilla Cuthbert," she tried again, "we've known each other too many years to fall out over..."

Wait a second. Perhaps she was being too lenient here. Perhaps Marilla should shoulder some of the blame too. After all, Rachel had been ill. She had not been fully responsible for her actions. Her voice took on a more self-righteous tone. "Marilla Cuthbert, we were both wrong. But you were probably wronger than me. However, I'm prepared to forgive and forget..." Oh dear, here she was at the house already, and not a line properly rehearsed.

As Rachel stepped up to the front door, it flew open and Davy came hurtling out, almost knocking her over. He was gone before she could stop him.

Marilla and Dora came racing down the stairs

behind Davy. "Davy Keith," called Marilla. "You come right back here!" But Davy had vanished into thin air.

"What on earth have you been doing to the child, Marilla? He looks frightened out of his wits."

"We have to find him before Miss Carpenter comes," moaned Marilla, too upset by Davy's departure to greet her friend's arrival. "Otherwise, what on earth will she think?"

"She'll think this place is mad as Bedlam," said Rachel, setting her case down on the front step with a contented sigh. "Which it is and always will be. Amen. I'll help you look for him, if you like, Marilla."

"We don't need to look. I know where he's gone," piped up Dora. "He's gone to talk to Mama."

Over Dora's head, Marilla and Rachel exchanged glances. "Is the poor child raving or what, Marilla?" whispered Rachel.

They watched as the little girl ran to the back of the house and across the yard. She stopped outside the barn, waiting for them to follow.

As soon as they stepped inside the dark building they could hear Davy. His voice was coming from somewhere high up, near the beams of the roof.

"Hang Sara, anyway!" he wept. "I'll give her what for when I sees her! Only I ain't never gonna see her no more."

"Davy Keith!" Marilla craned her neck upwards, peering into the shadows. "What in heaven's name are you doing up there, child? Come down at once."

"Sara said this was heaven," sobbed Davy. "So I come up here lookin' for my Mama, see?" He had used the rickety ladder to clamber onto the very top of the hay-pile, which ended just below one of the high barn windows.

"Don't cry, though, Davy, please!" Marilla felt close to tears herself.

"What else can I do? Mrs. Wiggins says I'm too young to swear. 'Sides, I gotta find my Mama. She'll save me from bein' tarred and feathered!"

Rachel started. She had completely forgotten about her bad-tempered threat and that awful scene with Davy before she left Green Gables. She stepped forward cautiously. "Davy," she said, then stopped. For some reason, she felt a large lump in her throat. She swallowed. "Forgive me for being such an old crab apple, Davy," she said. "I was wrong about you, I see that now." Tears pricked at her eyes. "You're not bad. You're not a rapscallion or a criminal neither. You're just a poor orphan boy who needs a good home and someone to love you and care for you. And Marilla and I intend to do just that."

Behind her she heard a gasp from Marilla. But her attention was focused on the little boy. She could see him now, his round face smudged with tears, leaning forward to look down at her from behind a huge mound of hay.

In the darkness, Davy gulped back his sobs and listened. Never before had he heard a soft word from Rachel Lynde. He wanted to be quite sure that the voice speaking to him now really belonged to her.

"You mean you won't tar and feather me after all? You mean, you *like* me?" In his surprise and eagerness he scrambled forward.

"Watch out, Davy!" screamed Rachel, for the hay had toppled over, sending Davy flying down. In that brief second, both Marilla and Rachel knew that if he survived, they would never, never part with him again. Both closed their eyes and prayed.

When they opened them again, Dora and Davy were jumping together on the lowest tier of the hayloft, onto which Davy had fallen. Rushing forward, the two women grasped both children in their arms so joyously and so clumsily that they all fell back together onto the sweet-smelling hay in a jumbled heap.

The sun, which had been climbing steadily in the sky, reached the first of the two small windows that stared at each other across the top of the loft. Peering in, it pointed a dusty finger at the group below. Davy looked up, feeling its warmth on his face.

"Say, maybe Sara's right. Maybe heaven's up there after all. Only I couldn't see 'cause it was dark."

"I can see you've a lot to learn in the theology department," muttered Rachel, brushing the straw out of his hair.

A prim cough startled them all. Into the pool of light in which they sat walked a thin, gray figure. "Miss Cuthbert?" it said, blinking in the brightness. "I'm Miss Carpenter. From the orphanage."

Marilla sat up straight, a look of horror on her face. Hay clung to her blouse and hair. She shook her head, but no words came out.

"I can certainly see what you meant about these children being too much for you at your age," the woman commented. Although the words were sympathetic, her tone was not. "I'm sure I can find a more suitable home for them elsewhere."

Rachel got to her feet, pulled down her jacket and straightened her skirts. Walking right up to Miss Carpenter, she stared her straight in the eye. Miss Carpenter coughed a tiny cough and stepped back a pace, out of the light.

"Now listen here, my good woman." There was a dangerous quiver in Rachel's tone. "I'll thank you not to throw my friend's age in her face! Marilla Cuthbert is a strong and capable woman, and I, her lifelong friend, do not intend to sit idly by and allow her to hand over these children to strangers."

Miss Carpenter blinked. "I thought..." She turned helplessly to Marilla. "Am I to understand—?"

"Anyone with half a mind can see these children belong here," interrupted Rachel. "Would you speak up, Marilla, and tell her so yourself?"

Marilla struggled to her feet, pulling both children after her. She looked directly at Miss Carpenter. "I'm sorry to bring you out on a wild goose chase, Miss Carpenter, but yes, my friend Rachel Lynde is right. The children stay here."

"Right here," repeated Rachel, "where they belong."

But she might as well have saved her breath to cool her porridge, for her words were drowned beneath the delighted screams of Davy and Dora.

Later that day, Marilla and Rachel sat together on the veranda, sharing tea and memories.

"I'd like to think I'm not one of them as won't give credit where credit is due, Marilla," confessed Rachel, putting down her cup. "If it hadn't been for your advice, all those many years ago, I might have married Ambrose Dinsdale." She smiled. "Me and dozens of others!"

"If ever anybody loved you truly, it was Thomas Lynde," replied Marilla.

"I know, and I'll spend the rest of my life thanking God for him." Reaching into her reticule, Rachel brought out the faded photograph of Ambrose and his lock of hair. In one swift motion, she had scattered the hair to the wind. Then she tore the photograph into little pieces. "Good riddance to bad rubbish!" she said, dropping tiny fragments of Ambrose into the wastebasket.

"Please, Mrs. Lynde, what's this?" demanded Davy. Growing bored with helping Dora shell peas, he had wandered over to their table, holding something whitish in his hand.

"That's Rachel's tooth, Davy," smiled Marilla. "We're going to preserve it for posterity. So put it back in its jar."

"Say, you think it might fit me?" asked Davy.

Rachel's thoughts flitted back to the day of Davy's mother's funeral, when her tooth had first begun to ache badly. She remembered the searing pain and her conviction that a wasp had lodged in her jaw. How long ago it all seemed, and how foolish she had been not to go to Dr. Blair sooner! She had to admit, too, that she had been wrong about the twins. They fitted in very nicely at Green Gables. Why, even Davy seemed to be settling down.

"Oh no, Davy Keith!" she heard Marilla moan. "What have you done?"

Rachel snapped to attention. Strange strangling noises issued from Davy's throat. He had turned white.

"What is it, child?" she gasped.

"Don't be mad," gargled Davy. "I was jes' tryin that tooth a yours on fer size. Only I burped, see and swallowed it. Say..." He brightened up. "Do you think it might meet up with my conscience on the way down? I want to know."

Rachel and Marilla exploded in laughter.

"As for that Mr. Grapple," resumed Rachel, when they had wiped their eyes. "He's no better than Ambrose Dinsdale, if you ask me. I intend to drop *him* like an old glove. With two children to raise, we won't have time for funerals."

Smiling contentedly, the two old friends bustled into the kitchen. They had a meal to prepare. It was their first meal together as a new and happy family and they intended to make it live in the children's memory forever.